finally sure

Laurel
Shadrach
series
5

finally
sure

stephanie perry moore

Moody Publishers
CHICAGO

Library of Congress Cataloging-in-Publication Data

Moore, Stephanie Perry.
   Finally sure / Stephanie Perry Moore.
      p. cm. — (Laurel Shadrach series ; bk. 5)
   Summary: During the latter part of Laurel's freshman year at college,
she makes decisions regarding her personal salvation.
   ISBN 0-8024-4039-8
   [1. Salvation—Fiction. 2. Colleges and universities—Fiction. 3.Christian life—Fiction.] I. Title.

PZ7.M788125Fi 2004
[Fic]—dc22

                                                                        2003019832

1 3 5 7 9 10 8 6 4 2

Printed in the United States of America

For my maternal grandfather,
James Murphy Roundtree
(1919–1971)

Though I was only two
when you went on to be with God,
your loving memory
has been with me all my life.

I'm passing on to my girls
your legacy of endearing love,
strong family, and blissful happiness.

FINALLY let me say,
your wife and children miss you,
but I'm SURE
we'll all see you soon.
The Jesus that was in your heart
is in ours as well.

contents

acknowledgments

Well, it was a hard day for my family and me today. We laid my 82-year-old grandmother to rest. It's tough because I wasn't expecting her to leave us so soon. I know you might think 82 years is a long time. Well, my granddad is 89 and he's still here. I guess losing a dear friend at any time is painful, whether you expect it or not. So if you've lost a loved one, I feel for you.

But hold on, I do have good news. Because, though my heart still aches, my soul is rejoicing. See, I know *Mrs. Lizzie Mae Dennis* is with God. Yeah, she can't sing me all her songs, teach my little girls how to play the piano, or make me her famous tea anymore; but what a relief it is to imagine her singing in the heavenly choir, and to think of her teaching anyone who wants to learn how to play sweet notes on the gold, grand piano, and to just see her having tea with her own grandmas. Actually, God's Word says Heaven is unimaginable. So it's got to be even better than that. What comfort and peace it is to know God has prepared a wonderful place for all of us who know Him.

So, if you lost someone who knew the Lord, be happy because they are in great hands. If you know friends who aren't saved, make sure you witness to them so that they won't be eternally separated from God. The funeral of the unsaved person is definitely a dreadful ending. If you are a believer and think being a teen is tough sometimes, be excited because it will all be worth it in the end. God is not through with you yet!

You may leave this world young, you may leave later in life, or you may be here when Jesus comes back for His bride. Whichever time is yours, know that it is coming. And just as when we receive warning that a great storm is on the way we prepare, so too do you also need to be prepared for the day the heavenly roll is called. If you want true happiness, joy, and peace, make sure that you know the Lord for yourself. Our reward is yet to come and I'll look to celebrate with you there.

To everyone who helps me spread the message of salvation: My parents, Dr. Franklin and Shirley Perry, Sr.; my publishing company, Moody Publishers, particularly Amy Peterson; my reading pool—Kathleen Hanson, Sarah Hunter, Laurel Kasay, Carol Shadrach, and Marietta Shadrach; my assistants, Nakia Austin, Nicole Duncan, Courtney Manning, and Ashley Morgan; to my Greek resource person, Adria Kimbrough; my paternal grandpa, Rev. Dewey E. Perry (who inspires me as he carries on without Grandma) and my maternal grandma, Mrs. Viola Roundtree (whose strength impresses me as she's lived years without her husband); my daughters, Sydni and Sheldyn; my husband, Derrick Moore; and most importantly, my Savior, Jesus Christ—my belief in You saves my soul. *Because of your prayers, I know this novel will cause a lot of young people to make sure more people are saved.*

o N e

wanting
only peace

it was such a joy being back in Conyers, Georgia, for the holidays. I loved college, but sometimes I missed being at home with my family.

"I am so in love with You, Lord," I said to the dimly lit sky as I leaped up off the frozen ground in front of my parents' home. It was Christmas Eve and I was going to be happy even though my life wasn't perfect.

I had just heard the news that my paternal grandfather had had a stroke. I didn't have a boyfriend. I knew I probably wouldn't make my college gymnastics team. But none of that really mattered.

I did want my grandfather to be OK, of course, especially since he wasn't saved. His salvation was really important to me, so I prayed that Granddad Shadrach would receive God into his heart.

It had taken eighteen and a half years, but I was finally

getting to the place where I was comfortable with myself and satisfied with my relationship with the Lord.

As a cold breeze played with my long brown hair, I started dancing in the snow. Come what may, I knew I didn't have to fear anything because I was a child of the King. I could practically hear God's voice in the wind, telling me He loved me.

"Yes, Lord," I shouted, letting the cold air kiss my face. "I love You too!"

Although I was by myself, I was not dancing alone. God was twirling me in His arms.

As the howling wind whisked me around, I felt the Lord saying to me, *I'm so proud of you, Laurel. This last year and a half has been tough. But I'm here. I love you. I love all the people in the world. Make sure you share that with everyone you know.*

My friends sure did need the Lord. All of them were going through some sort of drama. My best friend, Brittany, had been HIV positive for almost a year. She seemed to have the disease under control, though, and I hoped things would remain that way. Meagan, my other close high school buddy, had recently learned she was pregnant and decided to take a semester off to have the baby. Robyn, my African-American friend, was depressed about having had an abortion, and she wanted to change schools to be near Jackson Reid, her aborted baby's father. I thought her reason for changing colleges was a bad one, but I prayed her transition would be smooth.

My family was in chaos too. My dad, who was a pastor and a really cool guy, was upset about his father dying of cancer, especially since Granddad didn't know the Lord. My dad had been kinda taking things out on my mom, which really bothered me.

The older two of my three brothers, Liam and Lance, were still mad at each other over my friend Meagan, whom they had both dated for a while.

Liam, who was a year younger than me, was very talented.

He loved music and led the church youth band. Liam's biggest problem was that he was judgmental. He thought he was almost as perfect as God. Not!

Lance, who was a year younger than Liam, was a ladies' man. Or so he wished. He was actually a sports jock and sort of a hothead, always starting brawls.

My youngest brother, Luke, had been a computer geek all his life. After he started high school a year ago, he became cooler. But that was leading to a whole different set of problems.

With all the difficulties of my friends and family weighing on my heart, I had decided to come outside to be alone with God, to let Him know how I felt and seek guidance from Him.

As I listened to His response in my spirit, I knew He was telling me that I had to trust Him. I needed to always be satisfied with Him. He wanted me to have peace in my heart, even if there wasn't peace in my circumstances.

That's what I longed for too. I didn't want to let the crazy world dictate my life. I could be peaceful if I kept my eyes on the Lord. I could be the calm center in a tornado, a light in darkness.

At that moment I felt so close to God, I wanted to remember this night with Him always.

Lord, I love You so much! And I know You love me. All I need is You. Please don't let me forget that. When the storms come, and I know they will, help me stay calm. Let me carry You with me always.

When I stepped back inside the house, I heard my three brothers arguing. I couldn't tell what they were upset about. But as soon as I walked into their room, their verbal disagreement turned into a physical fight.

Liam and Lance started rolling around on the floor like idiots. Luke just stood there watching.

"What's going on in here?" I asked my youngest brother.

"We were all talking about how none of us wants to go

to Granddad and Grandma's house, and it turned into this."
Luke stepped out of the way as our wrestling brothers came
crashing toward us.

"Stop it, y'all," I hollered.

Lance and Liam acted like they hadn't even heard me.
They just pulled each other up off the floor and started
pounding on each other.

I turned to Luke. "Help me break this up." I tried to pry
the fighters apart, but Lance shoved me to the side. I landed
on my bottom with a thud.

Luke grabbed his brothers' shoulders and tried to push
them apart. "They're like glue," he shouted over the racket.

Finally my parents marched into the room. Luke slipped
out as quiet as a shadow. Liam and Lance stopped fighting
as soon as they noticed Mom and Dad standing in the doorway, both with their arms crossed.

My mother demanded to know what was going on.
Liam stared at the floor, his left eye all red and puffy. Lance
tried to hold his ripped shirt closed. Obviously, neither one
wanted to answer Mom's question.

I decided to spill the beans for them. "They don't want
to go to Arkansas for Christmas."

I wished we didn't have to make the ten-hour drive, either, but we'd done it every year since we moved to Georgia
five years ago. When we were younger, the trip had been
fun. But now that we each had our own life, we all preferred
spending our time hanging out with friends.

Mom glared at Dad. "This is all your fault. I told you the
kids didn't want to go to your parents' house this year, but
you wouldn't listen to me."

"What are we supposed to do?" my dad said, raising his
palms. "We obviously can't leave them here, not with the
way they're acting."

Mom gently touched Dad's shoulder. "Dave," she said
softly, "I don't see why the boys have to go if they don't want
to."

"We're all going and that's final," my dad said. Then he stomped down the hall, with Mom right behind him.

My dad's stern voice sent shock waves through me. He usually referred to my mother with some term of affection like honey, sweetie, or baby. I almost never heard him yell at her.

"It's gonna be a great trip," I mumbled.

Liam stalked down the hall to the bathroom and slammed the door. Lance jumped on his bed and turned his back to me. Clearly there wasn't anything I could do at that moment to resolve this mess. So I went to my room and knelt by my bed.

Being light in darkness is really hard sometimes, Lord, I prayed. *Please show me how to respond as You would.*

That night, I dreamed about Charlie, my college library partner whom I'd grown fond of. In the dream, he and I were running away from a bunch of enormous dinosaurs. The T-Rex was gaining on us when an angry voice startled me awake.

"Why didn't you pack all that stuff last night?" my dad roared from his bedroom. "I guess I have to do everybody's job around here."

It was only two in the morning. *What is going on with my father?* I wondered.

I knew some ministers acted one way in church and a different way in the world, but with my dad, what you saw in church was always what you got.

I'd noticed a change in him lately, though. Something was wrong. I wondered if he was even more worried than I was about his father's physical and spiritual health.

Within a few moments, everyone in the house was rushing around getting ready to leave. My dad was yelling and pouting about his schedule being off. Personally, I didn't see why we had to leave so early. A few hours later wouldn't have made much difference, it seemed to me.

I could tell my mother was mad, as I saw her roll her eyes and bite her bottom lip. But she didn't disagree with him. She simply finished packing.

I wasn't sure I agreed with the way my mom just went along with whatever my dad wanted. If the Lord ever allowed me to be someone's wife, the whole submission thing would be a gray area for me. Where was my mom's backbone? Where was her strength?

When I got my own suitcase packed, I carried it downstairs and dropped it near the front door, then went into the kitchen, where Mom was packing a cooler with ice.

Remember, you're a light, my heart said. *Be a light to your mom.*

"Need help?" I asked.

She stopped and gave me a big hug. "The cooler's all filled," she said after our embrace. "Can you check on the boys, see if they're ready?"

"Sure."

As I went back upstairs, I said a silent prayer for my dad. He had never reacted to stress so crazily before. Then again, his father had never been severely ill before. If my dad ever had a stroke, who knew how I'd react. Since I wasn't walking in his shoes, I couldn't judge how he was wearing them.

An hour later, we were all in the van. Dad still looked mad, but he'd stopped yelling, so my brothers and I went back to sleep.

When I woke up, Liam was in the driver's seat. His swollen eye had turned black, red, and purple.

We pulled into McDonald's at our usual halfway point a little after 8 A.M. Unfortunately, we still had five more hours to go. After using the restroom and getting some breakfast, we continued to drive west.

When we finally arrived in Arkansas, we went straight to the hospital. My father had called ahead to see how Granddad was doing and what room he was in.

16

A nurse at the reception desk told us only three visitors at a time were allowed, and Grandma was already in there. So my brothers and I waited in the lobby while our parents took off down the hall.

I stared at the light blue walls, the magazines on the tables, and the small television in one corner near the ceiling. Lance and Liam sat in a couple of plastic chairs near the TV, and Luke sprawled out on a small couch in the opposite corner. Before I could decide where I wanted to sit, I heard my grandpa's voice.

"Why did you let them come out here? I'm fine, I tell you! Why do you always have to mess up everything?"

A nurse left her station and scurried down the hall. As she entered a room, I saw my grandma coming out. Her face was white and tears streamed down her cheeks. She fled down the hall, past the lobby, and continued along the corridor.

My brothers and I stared at one another. Then I took off in the direction Grandma had run. When I reached the end of the hall, I looked left and right. No sign of my grandmother. I went right for a while, but didn't see her, so I backtracked.

I finally found her in the chapel. She was sitting in the front pew facing the altar, her head in her hands. I tiptoed down the aisle and stood beside her, stroking her back. Her head remained bowed, and I heard her sniffling.

I sat beside her. *Lord, what am I supposed to say?*

The chapel door opened. We both turned around. My dad stood in the doorway. "Come on, Laurel," he said, his voice strained. "We're going to Grandma's. Granddad doesn't want us here."

I looked at my grandma and saw tears in her eyes.

"Mom, we'll see you back at the house," Dad muttered.

Hesitantly, I left my grandma's side. When I got to the door of the chapel, I turned around and saw my grandmother kneeling at the altar, praying softly.

It was Christmas Day. All I wanted was to give my grandfather a hug, make sure he knew Jesus, go to my grandparents' house, eat a big family meal, and thank God for sending His Son, Jesus Christ, to die on the cross for my sins. But it sure wasn't working out that way, and there was nothing I could do about it.

We all piled back into the van. My father drove with an angry expression on his face. My mother sat in the passenger seat looking sad. My brothers acted as if they would rather be anywhere else in the world.

"We didn't have to leave the hospital," my mom said to my dad in a soft, concerned voice.

"With my father carrying on the way he was, I didn't see any point in staying," Dad said. "We drove all this way and he told us to get out. We just have to let him cool off. We'll be at the house when he's ready to talk to us."

"But your mother needed us," Mom persisted, "and we just left her there."

Dad sighed. "Laura, these are my parents, and I've got to handle this the way I see fit."

My mother's lips tightened and she stared out the window.

"I can't believe my father was fussing at my mom like that," Dad grumbled.

"Why not?" Lance rebutted angrily. "You're fussing at Mom."

Dad swerved the van to the side of the road, slammed on the brakes, and turned around. "I am tired of your smart mouth, young man, and I'm sick of your defiant behavior."

"Just following your lead, Dad," Lance said. "Look in the mirror before you come after me."

I leaned slightly left, figuring my father was going to take a swing at Lance and maybe get me on the way by. But he just sat there, staring at his son. After several deep breaths, Dad turned back around, put the car into drive, and took off down the road.

I reached over to hold my brother's hand, but he yanked it away.

With three generations of Shadrach men filled with rage, and no one sympathizing with one another, I knew somehow, some way, that cycle had to be broken. It was Christmas, after all. And this family definitely needed the Savior.

Lord, I wondered, *how can this be fixed?*

I wished I was back at college. I wanted to talk to Charlie, the sweet, mysterious guy I'd met in the library. He really seemed to understand me. Nothing romantic was going on between us, although I wondered if our friendship might turn into something more. I missed him and wished he was there beside me so I could tell him what was going on and he could give me some good Christian advice.

I didn't even know his real name, and he didn't know mine. The first time we met, we'd given each other pet names—Charlie and Lucy, after the *Peanuts* comic-strip characters—and the names had stuck.

I remembered dancing with the Lord the night before, confident that God was all I needed. I knew I had to have His help to get through this mess with my family.

I took the box of tissues off the seat beside me and handed it to my mother. She accepted it with a smile that let me know hope was around the corner. God had His eye on my family. I just had to stay calm in the midst of the storm. I needed to trust in Him.

My mom's parents lived a few miles away from my dad's folks, so Dad dropped us off at my maternal grandparents' house and then took off. We were welcomed with open arms and big hugs from my grandmother, my grandfather, and my Aunt Sara, Mom's only sister.

As I looked around my grandparents' house, I noticed my Aunt Sara's furniture mixed in with the things I was used to seeing there. The old rocking chair still stood in the usual corner of the living room, but cardboard boxes were scattered around it. My aunt's six-piece set of Gucci luggage sat near the doorway, and my cousin's CD collection was stacked up behind Grandma's antique couch.

I sat on the couch and grabbed the gray afghan off the back. As always, it gave me a cozy feeling inside.

After my brothers went to the back room to wash up for dinner, my grandmother sat beside me. "Laurel, dear," she said, patting my knee, "it's so good to see you."

"Why are Aunt Sara's things here?" I asked.

"She and the girls are staying with us." The seriousness in her voice made me think my aunt was there for more than just the holidays.

I had two cousins on my mom's side. Simone was seventeen, a year younger than me. She had big hazel eyes and long blonde hair. She was sarcastic and outspoken, could never keep a secret, and loved to start arguments.

Rebecca, on the other hand, was polite and sweet. She was nineteen, a year older than me, a sophomore at Arkansas. She was incredibly beautiful with long honey-blonde hair and bright blue eyes.

"I know you and Simone don't always get along," my grandmother said, "but I don't want you to fuss at her this visit. Their family is going through a tough time right now." She lowered her voice to a whisper. "Sara's getting a divorce."

My heart practically leaped out of my chest. I felt like part of my insides were sliding away.

Grandma gave me a hug and then went out to the kitchen to start getting dinner on the table. As I walked into the family room, I saw Becca and Simone sitting on a love seat watching TV. I wanted to ask them about their parents' divorce. But I decided to keep my nose in my own business and went to the bathroom to wash my hands.

We all gathered around the dinner table, the parents and

grandparents at one end and my brothers, cousins, and I at the other. Every person there seemed to have a sad look on his or her face. But the spread my grandmother had prepared smelled heavenly. I hoped the turkey and side dishes would brighten everyone's spirits.

The dinner conversation was light at first. Our grandparents got updates on how we all were doing. Not wanting to worry them, I only shared my high points. They were glad to hear my transition to college had been a smooth one.

While the conversation continued at the far end of the dining table, Becca whispered to me, "Where's your dad?"

"I'm not sure," I said, shrugging my shoulders. "He's been pretty moody lately. Hopefully he went somewhere to cool off."

Simone's lips curled into a smirk. "Hey, maybe your parents will split up like ours."

I felt like snapping at her. But I remembered Grandma's warning not to fuss with her. So I concentrated on my food and ignored her hurtful words.

"Weekend visitation is actually pretty cool," Simone said as she took a second helping of mashed potatoes. "Dad always takes us to the mall. He never did that when he lived with us."

Becca tossed back her hair. "Come on, Simone. You know you don't want her parents to end up like ours."

While I listened to my cousins argue, I prayed that whatever was causing their parents to break up would reverse itself before the divorce became final.

At the far end of the table, I heard my mother saying encouraging words to her sister. I was proud of my mom. In the midst of her own strife, she was still compassionate toward others. My mom was one unselfish lady.

The doorbell rang, and my grandfather got up to answer it. When I saw my dad standing at the door, I jumped up and ran toward him.

"Son," I heard my grandfather say sternly, "I have never interfered in your marriage. But this afternoon my baby came to my house in tears. Now, you need to take care of her properly."

"You're right, sir," my father said, his voice filled with remorse. "I'm sorry."

My grandfather shook my dad's hand and stepped back so he could enter the house. When my dad saw me, he hugged me. Then I returned to my seat.

My dad was a proud man, but he never minded admitting when he was wrong. He came into the dining room, apologized for interrupting our dinner, and looked into my mom's eyes. "I'm sorry for being such a jerk," he said right in front of everybody. "Please forgive me, honey."

Mom immediately rose and hugged my father.

Dad glanced at our end of the table. "Kids, I owe you an apology too. You were right, Lance. I was mad at my father for doing something I was guilty of myself. I was so agitated and frustrated, I couldn't see it. Thanks for helping me realize that I was wrong."

My brothers and I cheered.

My father sat next to my mom and she fixed him a plate. "Dad's out of the hospital," he announced, "and he'd really like to see all of us."

We rejoiced at Granddad's change of heart. After dinner was over, we said good-bye to Aunt Sara and her daughters and hopped back into the car.

When we got to my other grandparents' house, we all scrambled inside and embraced my grandma. My dad's father called us to his room. My parents and I went back while my brothers waited in the living room with Grandma.

I found my grandpa propped up in bed, watching television in his pajamas. Since he'd only had a light stroke, he looked almost like his usual self, just a little paler and tired.

He picked up the remote, clicked off the program, and looked each of us in the eye. "Saying I'm sorry isn't my cup of tea," he stammered. "But I want you guys to know I'm happy you're here." He gave a small chuckle. "I'm glad I'm still here too."

We all hugged him and told him how much we loved him. Then Granddad said, "Y'all go back to the family room and enjoy the holiday."

My folks squeezed his hand and cleared out, but I couldn't leave. I just stood there staring at my grandfather. His life had been spared, but what if his time to go was just around the corner? If he didn't ask the Lord to come into his heart before he died, he'd be going to hell. I needed to tell him that.

"Pudding Pie," he said, trying to keep the mood light, "I know you want to talk to me about God, and I love you for caring about me. But I'm an old man, set in my ways."

"Granddad, you're alive," I said, tears stinging my eyes. I hoped he realized that the Lord had spared his life. "You still have a chance to accept the Lord. Don't wait till it's too late."

He rubbed my hand. "I'm too tired to argue with you right now. But I'm OK, believe me. Now get out there with the rest of the family."

I kissed him on the forehead and sulked out of the room. It hurt to leave him without having him accept Christ.

I trudged back to the living room and found my brothers and my dad watching TV. My mother and Grandma were in the kitchen making apple pie. As I took a whiff of the delectable aroma, I felt God's presence and peace.

My dad saw me in the hallway and waved me over to him. Smiling, I sat beside him on the couch. He took my hand. "I overheard you in there witnessing to your grandpa. Don't be discouraged, honey. The Lord's working in his heart."

"I know," I said quietly.

"I'm really proud of you, Laurel," he said. "You love God and you don't care who knows it."

My mom came in and sat with us. Dad gave her a big kiss. It was sweet seeing them all romantic.

During dessert, my brothers were so nice to one another, it was like nothing bad had happened. After we ate our fill, the whole family gathered around the piano to sing Christmas carols.

As I sang, I realized my dad was right. Things weren't the way I wanted them to be, but they were good. This was the anniversary of the day Christ was born, and that was something to celebrate. I also had close family who would help me weather any storm.

Our family didn't open any presents that night. But we all had the gift of happiness. At the end of the day, all was well in the Shadrach family. I thanked the Lord for that. He had given me the best gift I could ever receive. For the last twenty-four hours I had been wanting only peace.

hoping
in Him

after the interesting Christmas Day with my family in Arkansas, I was happy to get back home. I looked forward to having a few days to relax before going back to my dorm at UGA. As I lay in my cozy bed, the ringing of my phone startled me. Payton's frazzled voice on the line startled me even more.

"Why are you crying?" I asked her.

She was sobbing so much she couldn't speak.

"Please tell me what's wrong. You're scaring me."

"I'm here in Conyers," she finally choked out. "I haven't left to go back to school yet."

"Is everything OK?"

"My family's ripped apart," she said. "Our head is gone."

I didn't know if I'd heard her wrong or if she was crying so much that I couldn't follow her. She might have been talking slang that I didn't understand. See, Payton was a sweet black girl who loved God and loved life. Hearing her down made me know something had to be really wrong with my strong friend.

"I was the last person who talked to him," Payton went on. "He was here and now he's not. I mean, it's a good thing to know you're going to heaven, but this is too much."

"Your father's gone?" I asked, trembling. I'd be hurt deeply if I lost my dad, even though I knew the Lord would help me get through it.

"Not my father," Payton explained. "His dad."

I could easily imagine Granddad passing away after visiting him at the hospital. "I'm sorry," I said. "But your grandfather was a strong Christian. So even though he's absent from the body, he's present with the Lord."

"But, Laurel, he's gone." Her deep sobs told me my words hadn't been much comfort to her.

"I know," I said, wishing I could hug her. "But he's in a much better place. He wouldn't come back here if he could. You're going to see him again. And when we all get to heaven, I'll get to meet him too."

She paused. "I don't know how I'm gonna get through his funeral."

I clutched the phone. "God will get you through it. I'll be praying for you."

"Thanks, Laurel. You're a good friend."

"When is the service?" I asked.

"This afternoon."

I heard someone call Payton's name and she said she had to go, so she told me quickly where and when the service would be held, then we hung up.

I went downstairs to my dad's study to see if he would go to the funeral with me. When I saw him pacing and reading, rehearsing for Sunday's sermon, I lingered in the doorway. He'd been swamped ever since we returned from Arkansas, so I didn't want to disturb him.

My father stopped pacing when he realized I was in the room. "What do you need, honey?"

"Nothing urgent," I said. "I can talk to you later when you're not so busy."

He put down his sermon notes. "I always have time for you." He pointed to a chair and took a seat behind his desk. "What's going on?"

My dad could always tell when I needed to speak to him about something important. I rushed around his desk and hugged him tight. I wanted my dad to know he meant a lot to me.

"What's that for?" he asked as we let go of the embrace.

Tears came to my eyes. "Payton's grandfather . . ."

"He passed?" my dad guessed.

I wiped my eyes with my hands. "Yeah."

"Where does Payton's grandmother live?"

"Here in Conyers." I fell into the mahogany chair on the opposite side of his desk.

"Are you going to the funeral?"

"I want to." I wished this was all a bad dream. "But I'd rather not go alone."

"I'll go with you."

I stared at him. "But you're so busy."

With a warm smile, he said, "I'll make the time."

A few hours later I was sitting in a small Baptist church with my hand clasped firmly in my dad's. I couldn't believe he was able to come with me on such short notice, but he kept his word and made the time. I was thankful he was there.

Payton's family took up the first five pews on both sides of the church. Payton sat on the front pew with her head held high, so she appeared to have outer strength. She looked around to see who was in the crowd. When she saw me, I smiled, and she smiled back through her tears.

The mood was sad but not without hope. Payton's grandfather's heart was right with God, so we knew he was in a better place.

I wanted desperately to tell my grandfather one more time what Jesus had done for him. He needed to accept Christ into his heart so He could wash his sins away.

As I watched Payton's grandfather's body lying in an open casket in the front of the church, I felt God confirming to my heart, *He's with Me, Laurel. Tell Payton her grandfather is with Me.*

A choir sang "Precious Lord," then the pastor gave a sermon.

"We weep today because we are saddened by the departure of a loved one," the pastor said. "But this man accepted Jesus as his Savior, and he is now sitting next to God in heaven, happier than he ever was here on earth. He encouraged people to keep the faith. He knew God could heal wounded hearts."

As the pallbearers pushed the coffin into the hearse, I hurried to Payton's side and hugged her tight. "Don't worry. Your grandfather's with God. He's happy, so take comfort in that."

"Thanks," Payton said. She embraced me, then joined her family.

Two of my best friends from high school, Brittany and Meagan, stopped by my house the next morning. We sat in my room and chatted, mostly about Meagan's unwanted pregnancy. She had decided to give the child up for adoption. But Brittany thought that was a bad idea.

"I don't see how you can just give up your baby," my pretty blonde friend said as she sat on my bed.

Meagan lay beside Brittany with her hand behind her head. "At least I didn't get an abortion. Giving my baby to strangers is better than ending his life."

I sat beside Meagan and glared at Brittany. "Meagan's right. She made a mistake, but she's trying to do the right thing. She's willing to make a sacrifice so her child can have a better life than she can give it. You've done bad things in your life, too, and I'm not perfect either. We've all made mistakes. Let's be there for her."

Brittany gave me an angry frown. "What happens when the kid hunts Meagan down one day and asks, 'Mom, how could you just give me up to people you didn't even know? Didn't you love me? How could you do that? Didn't you care?' "

"I'm sure my child will ask me those questions one day," Meagan said, holding her head high. "If he . . . or she . . . ever . . . finds me." She rolled over and shoved her face into the pillow. "Oh, what am I doing?"

I touched her trembling shoulder. "You're putting your baby in God's hands. Bethany Christian Services will find a wonderful family for your baby. My dad says they're excellent."

Sighing, Meagan sat up. "You're right. I can let God be there for my baby."

"I'm sorry, Meagan," Brittany said. "I didn't mean to make you sad."

"It's OK," Meagan said, taking Brittany's hand. "I know you had my best interest at heart."

Brittany sprang to her feet. "I've got a great idea. Let's go somewhere fun to eat, then come back here, and I'll paint your fingernails and toes."

Brittany always had her nails done at a salon, so offering to do our nails at home was her way of saying she was sorry. When tears fell from Meagan's eyes, I knew she was accepting Brittany's support.

"You're my hero," Brittany said, hugging Meagan.

"I love you," Meagan responded.

Brittany apologized to Meagan probably fifty more times that afternoon. I knew that Brittany finally understood this whole thing when she said God was in our midst doing a great work by cleaning up the mess we'd made along the way. She talked about her own life and said she was glad the

AIDS virus had been detected early. She'd changed her lifestyle from being promiscuous to abiding by the Lord's wishes, taking her medication daily, getting a lot of exercise, and starting to think positively.

Meagan said she was glad she could bless a family some-where with her baby. I admired her strength to place the child's needs above her own.

I began thinking about my high school boyfriend Branson and how I'd let him go a little too far with me. Now I was starting to have romantic feelings about the guy I'd met in the library. The guy I called Charlie was cute, funny, and intelligent. But I didn't know if he felt the same way about me, so I'd been suppressing my feelings and looking for signs from him.

As we got up to go to dinner, I hesitated. For some reason I couldn't understand, I just didn't feel like hanging out with my friends.

"What's wrong?" Brittany asked me.

"Nothing," I said with a shrug. "I just don't feel like going out after all. You guys go ahead."

"Laurel," Meagan pouted.

"What a party pooper," Brittany said as she headed for the door.

"I think I just need to spend a little time alone with the Lord," I said. "Why don't you come back after dinner?"

"That's cool," Brittany said. "Maybe we can have a sleepover."

"Great idea," I said.

We hugged and they left. As soon as I sprawled out on my bed to think and pray, the phone rang. It was Payton. She was still sad over her grandfather's passing, and I figured if I could get her to think about something else, that might distract her from her sorrow.

I invited her to come over, and she said she was up for spending the night at my place. After we hung up, I remembered I had other company coming over. The more I thought about Payton being in the same place as Brittany and Meagan, the more I panicked.

Payton had been through a whole bunch of turmoil with our suite mate, Jewels. Jewels was always making snide remarks about our belief in God, complaining when we spent too much time in the bathroom, telling us what was wrong with the way our room was arranged, and basically criticizing everything we did.

Jewels was a lot like Brittany. They were both beautiful and spoiled.

During our senior year of high school, Brittany had gone through a lot of tension when her dad started dating an African-American woman, who turned out to be the mother of Robyn Williams, a spunky African-American girl I'd met in one of my classes. They conspired to get together and break up their parents' relationship. In the end, they were successful. But after their parents' hearts were broken, they both felt bad. They hadn't talked to each other since.

I ran downstairs and found my mother in the kitchen making herself a grilled cheese sandwich. I wondered where Dad and my brothers were, then remembered they'd gone out to dinner together.

"Would you and your friends like something to eat?" Mom offered.

"Britt and Meagan went out," I said, "but I wasn't hungry."

"Are you feeling all right?" she asked, peering at me.

"I'm fine. I invited them to come back later for a sleepover."

"That's nice," Mom said, taking her sandwich off the griddle with a spatula.

"Payton asked to come over tonight too," I told her. "But I don't think Brittany and Meagan will get along with her very well."

As Mom took her plate to the kitchen table, she said, "They're all your friends. Maybe it's your role to unite them."

31

"Maybe," I said, trying to think of something they all had in common besides me.

"Why don't you pray about it," Mom suggested. "After all, the only approval you need is God's."

I kissed my mother on the cheek, thanked her, and ran back to my room. After praying about it for a while, I thought about my friend Robyn. She had gone to a historically black school. However, she'd told me she wanted to go to the University of Georgia the next year since that's where Jackson Reid, her ex-boyfriend was.

If Robyn came over, I figured, that might balance things out and maybe Payton wouldn't feel so out of place among all us white girls. Besides, if I introduced the two of them, Robyn could met someone from the college she was planning to attend.

I called Robyn and told her about my get-together.

"So," she teased, "you want me to come hang out with the black chick so you can spend time with your white friends."

"I just want her to feel comfortable." I explained that my roommate really needed a happy evening to combat her mourning.

Finally, Robyn said, "OK, I'll come. I ain't doing nothin' tonight anyway."

After we hung up, I spent the next two hours cleaning my room and putting out extra linen so my guests could sleep comfortably on my floor. Then I knelt by my bed, closed my eyes, and prayed.

Lord, I'm putting this night in Your hands. Be with us. Guide our thoughts. Five college freshmen with completely different issues are coming together. Let us enjoy each other and You. Thanks in advance for blessing our time. I love You, Lord.

The minute I finished praying, Robyn showed up in my bedroom doorway.

"I know I'm early. But I figured you might need help

cleaning up." She glanced around my room. "Dang! The place looks great."

She sat on my bed, and I shut my closet door. "Thanks for coming over on such short notice."

"Don't worry about it. I miss hanging out with you. Besides, maybe meeting your friend will be a blessing for me. I could use another sista."

When the doorbell rang I rushed to answer it. But when I opened the door and saw Brittany, Meagan, and Payton all standing there, and noticed the irritated look on Brittany's face and the confused look on Payton's, my chipper spirit vanished.

Robyn chuckled.

"Well," I said, "everyone follow me."

As I led them all up to my room, Brittany grabbed my arm and whispered, "Why do you have other people here? This was supposed to be our night to lift up Meagan."

I ignored her and kept walking. Everyone said hello to my mother as we passed her in the hallway.

When we got into my room, Brittany and Robyn stood by the window while Payton and Meagan sat on opposite sides of the bed. They all stared at me.

After taking a deep breath, I said, "I apologize for not telling you all that everyone else was coming. There was no secret plan. It just happened this way. So let's try to enjoy each other's company, OK?"

"I'm fine with that," Payton said. "I just need an introduction."

Everyone laughed and the tension faded away. I introduced everyone to Payton, and they all responded warmly.

As we chugged root beer and munched on popcorn while watching a movie on TV, I knew God had answered my prayers. The five of us were acting like we'd been friends since preschool. When I saw Payton smile during a funny part of the movie, I smiled too. My friend was going through pain but it was temporary.

Four of my dearest friends had a perfect evening together because I had prayed to an awesome God. I realized that hanging out with these ladies in heaven one day was something I definitely wanted to do. Winning souls for Christ was what my life was going to be about.

When I walked into the school library, I immediately took the elevator to the third floor, where I'd met the guy who'd been on my heart through the whole Christmas break. Charlie was seated at our usual table, focused on his studying. I strolled up to him and teased, "So, what's your name?"

Charlie looked up, stood, and placed his hands around my face. "I'm Stewart Little," he said jokingly, "and you're adorable. Kiss me."

"Laurel, wake up," Robyn said, waking me from my dream. "We're at Shoney's."

I looked around me and realized I was in a van with Payton, Robyn, Jackson, and his foster parents, Mr. and Mrs. Ford. As I shook the cobwebs out of my sleepy mind, I remembered we were on our way to the UGA bowl game. Georgia was going to play Michigan. Since the Fords were members of my dad's church, my folks had allowed me to go on the trip.

Jackson was supposed to ride with the team since he was part of the Georgia Bulldogs defense. However, the athletic department decided they could only fly down the playing squad, and Jackson was just a red-shirt freshman on the practice team. Once he got there, however, he'd be able to stay with the team.

During the whole ride, I'd felt weird vibes around me. Whenever Robyn wasn't looking, Jackson was flirting with Payton. I could tell Payton was irritated but didn't want to hurt her new friend Robyn. I was caught in the middle because Robyn was sitting next to me whispering about how much she wanted to be with Jackson.

When we arrived at the restaurant to get a quick bite to eat before the game, we all piled out of the van. Halfway through the parking lot, Payton said, "I left something in the car. You guys go ahead. I'll catch up."

After Payton turned back, Robyn started talking to me again about her feelings for Jackson. I wanted to tell her, *"Get a clue. He's not interested."* But I didn't want to break her heart.

When we finally reached the restaurant door, I looked back to see if Payton was coming. I noticed Jackson had followed her back to the van. I knew about Jackson's appetite. If he was willing to wait on food just so he could be with a girl, something was going on. However, I shook my head, knowing Payton could handle herself, and went inside to join the Fords and Robyn.

Robyn and I took a booth near the window. Jackson's foster parents sat a few tables down. Just as a young blonde waitress with "Carol" on her nametag arrived to take our order, Payton and Jackson came in and joined us. Payton was smiling, but her flared nostrils and tight mouth told me she was angry.

Half an hour later, we were eating our food. Jackson was rudely smacking on his sandwich. I wondered what he'd done to Payton. After he got Robyn pregnant in high school, he'd dumped her. He'd hit on me the following summer, even though he knew how close I was to Robyn. When I looked at Jackson eating a French fry and making goo-goo eyes with Robyn, I wished he would choke on that fry.

Jackson announced that he was going to the bathroom, and Robyn got up and followed him under the pretense that she had to use the restroom also. I figured she wanted to get him alone to give him a hint that she still liked him.

I looked at Jackson's foster parents. Mrs. Ford was feeding her husband some of her salad, and he laughed with every bite. She reached over to wipe a drop of dressing off his mouth, and he held her hand briefly. The love this couple displayed melted my heart.

God hadn't blessed them with children of their own, so they had opened their hearts to take in Jackson Reid, an at-risk African-American male who was eight years old at the time. Even then Jackson had exhibited aggressive behavior.

I knew not all African-American guys were troublemakers. Derek, a black Georgia Tech football player, had lived with us briefly, and he was a great Christian, nothing like Jackson Reid. Yet the Fords loved their foster son just as much as my parents loved me. They'd told several people at church that they'd become a more loving couple after going through all the struggles they had experienced together.

Payton touched my leg to get my attention. "I'm sick and tired of that boy," she whispered. "If he keeps messin' with me, he's gonna lose something he don't want to lose."

"Was he really coming on strong with you?" I asked.

"He wouldn't leave me alone," Payton said. "Kept tellin' me how good we'd be together. Really got on my nerves. He finally got the message when I told him flat out I wasn't interested. Now he's over there with Robyn, acting like he wants her." She pointed to the hallway near the restrooms, where Robyn and Jackson were standing close together. "If I'm ever that blind, slap me back into reality."

Payton was so heated I knew she needed God's strength to calm her down. So I held her hand and prayed.

As Robyn and Jackson came back to our table, the Fords came over too. "Laurel," Mr. Ford said, "I've watched you in church over the past few years, and your light has always shone bright for Christ. But seeing you and your friend praying right here in the restaurant, not caring what anyone else thinks about that, convicts me that I need to talk to God more myself."

"You need to talk to your trifling son, too," Payton mumbled. I gently kicked her under the table, and we shared a smile.

When we were all walking back to the van, I saw Jackson touch Payton's bottom. She raised her fist, but before she could make contact, Jackson dashed up to Robyn and placed his arm around her. Robyn smiled and turned to him for a peck on the cheek. Payton was livid.

I prayed for Payton as we drove to the hotel where the football team was staying. When Jackson got out of the van, Robyn and the Fords got out to say their good-byes to him. Payton and I stayed in the car.

When I saw Robyn give him a passionate embrace, I prayed silently, *Lord, please work all this out. Help Payton and Robyn's growing friendship to stay intact. Thanks for Your help, Lord.*

The next day, at the packed bowl game, all I could think about was Charlie. He was just my brother in Christ, my friend, and my study partner. I didn't want to fall for him, mainly because I was sure he only thought of me as a friend.

In spite of all the screaming fans, our team was losing badly. In the fourth quarter we were down by thirty points.

I felt sorry for the team—especially the kicker, Casey Hanson, who'd proclaimed in a school newspaper article that he was a Christian. I had empathized with him on several occasions throughout the football season. He was under a lot of pressure.

With less than two minutes to go, Hanson attempted a fifty-two-yard field goal. It bounced off the upright and veered outside the goalposts. The crowd booed him, which really aggravated me. He shuffled to the sideline, then took off his helmet and threw it on the ground.

I sent up a prayer to God to help him. The kicker was one of the bright lights on our pitiful Georgia Bulldogs team. If it wasn't for his points, we wouldn't have won the games we had. But on this particular day, none of his kicks went through the uprights.

I knew pouting on the sidelines wasn't what the Lord would want for Casey Hanson. So I prayed for him to be a witness in the midst of disappointment. In times of despair, God always wants us to keep our faith and keep hoping in Him.

trying
to adapt

"OK, girl, I'm going to fix you up," Robyn said to me at the bowl game. "It's obvious you're still into your ex."

Since Branson was the only guy Robyn knew I liked, she assumed I was praying passionately because of lingering feelings for him. She couldn't have been more wrong. Branson was the last guy on my mind. I was praying for the kicker.

My connection to Casey Hanson was something I'd never experienced before. It was like I was his prayer angel, and I knew God wanted me to lift him up.

Lord, help him, I prayed.

Casey looked like he really needed some divine help. I hoped my prayer would give him strength from the Lord so he could get some hope back in his step.

I turned to Robyn. "Don't worry about me. I'm fine."

The gleam in her eye told me she didn't believe me. She started scanning the program booklet and pointing out all the cute players.

After calling out the names of six or seven guys in the book she thought I'd be interested in, she cried, "Oh, Laurel, this one looks like your type."

When she said Casey Hanson's name, my heart skipped a couple of beats.

I felt tempted to sneak a peak at the kicker's picture, but kept my eyes averted. Though my heart didn't belong to Charlie, I did have feelings for him that could go somewhere, and I didn't want to taint that.

After the game Jackson's foster parents, Robyn, Payton, and I went to the Bulldog locker room to wait for the players to come out. I felt like a groupie. I was a big fan of my team, but I didn't want an autograph or a date or even a personal conversation with any of these guys, like some of the girls in the crowd obviously did. The team hadn't played a good game. Michigan killed us. I knew the coach would be telling the players they needed to take a cold, hard look at themselves because some big changes needed to happen.

I had no intention of undermining the coach's harsh words to the team by standing around telling them all they did great. I hadn't even wanted to go see the players after the game. But Payton and Robyn had dragged me along, and Jackson's parents wanted to say hi to their son. So I tagged along.

Jackson had spent the entire game on the sidelines. I couldn't imagine what his parents were going to say to him. "Way to go, Son; you held your helmet and wore your uniform well"?

Realizing that I was being harder on him than I should be because he'd been acting like such a jerk, I prayed that God would soften my sarcastic attitude toward him.

When Jackson came out of the locker room, instead of walking with his head hanging and shoulders drooped, he strutted over to us like he was the star quarterback. "Y'all can go on back home," he announced with a proud smile. "I'm flying back to school with the team."

Big deal, I thought.

"Coach said some of the players and administrators are hanging around here for a while since it's the holidays. There's space for me on the plane next week, so I'm gonna hang with my boys. That cool with you?" He gave his folks a look that was somewhere between puppy-dog pleading and *I'm an adult now, so you can't say no.*

"That's fine," Mr. Ford said as he pulled out his wallet and handed his son some cash. Jackson thanked his dad and gave his mom a hug.

When he started to say good-bye to Robyn, she tried to persuade him to change his mind and ride back with us. "We can sit in the backseat," she said, "and I can rub your ankles."

"No, thanks," he said casually. "I'd rather ride home with the team."

"Come on, baby," she urged, seductively playing with his cheek. "Why would you want to ride on a plane full of smelly guys when you could be with a woman like me?"

I hated seeing my friend humiliate herself. The Fords looked at her, and then at each other, a concerned expression on their faces.

Payton tugged on Robyn's arm and pulled her away from Jackson. He waved to us all, called out, "See ya," and strolled toward a group of giggling girls.

Robyn watched him talking to the other girls for a moment, then turned to me with a strained look of false confidence. "He just wants to hang with his friends. It's no big deal. I've gotta give him a little space."

"Are you gonna be OK?" I asked gently.

"I'm fine," she said.

I raised one eyebrow and shook my head.

"Don't look at me like that," she said. "I'm totally cool."

"You don't look cool," I said. "You look like your heart has been broken."

"It's not that serious," she said. "He'll come around someday and realize I'm the one for him."

I decided to let her put on the brave front. Besides, not having Jackson riding with us would mean a more peaceful drive. I just prayed my girlfriend would get a clue.

When Robyn and I started walking through the crowd in the tunnel, I saw Payton in Tad Taylor's arms. She'd dated him in high school, but she broke it off, and he found someone else once he got to college. She'd been sad about it, but she didn't beg him to come back to her. She let go of him and trusted God. I wished Robyn could do that.

When Tad released Payton and took off with his new girlfriend, Payton looked upset. I walked up beside her and hugged her. "It's gonna be OK."

"Yeah, I know," my roommate replied as she placed her arm around me.

Out of the corner of my eye, I saw a guy who looked like Charlie standing at the far end of the tunnel. "Oh, my gosh," I said, trying to get a better look. "Surely that's not . . ."

"Who?" Robyn asked.

I squinted into the shadows. The guy who looked like Charlie was wearing loose-fitting jeans, the latest kicks, and a gray turtleneck sweater. He was having a conversation with a blonde girl.

I started walking toward the guy, but Mrs. Ford called me and said it was time to leave. They headed back toward the van, and I had to follow.

Jackson's parents drove to the hotel they'd booked for us all to spend the night in. They had generously paid for a separate room for us girls that adjoined theirs.

After we all got settled in, I told Payton and Robyn, "We've got to find a way to be satisfied with just God. He has to fill us."

"Yeah, right, Laurel," Robyn teased. "What about that guy you were checking out before we left the game?"

"What are you talking about?" I asked, laying out my pajamas.

"I saw you looking at a guy," she said, "and it wasn't Branson. Who was it?"

"It doesn't matter. That's what I'm trying to say. I've decided to turn my dating relationships over to God. My hope is in the Lord, not in any guy."

"I totally agree," Payton said. "Only God can truly satisfy me. I need to get my relationship with Him straight. My passion needs to burn for Him alone."

Robyn shook her head and went into the bathroom. But I knew I'd given her something to mull over.

I smiled. *The three of us are going to be OK.* We had God, so we had everything.

"I've got this," Brittany told Meagan and me as she grabbed the check from the waiter. "Lunch is on me."

We were about to go back to our different worlds, living in three different places. I'd be headed to UGA. Brittany was going back to the University of Florida. And Meagan was going to stay in Conyers to have the baby.

"I don't know how I'm going to make it without you two," Brittany said.

My cute blonde friend was showing a vulnerable side I hadn't seen since she was first diagnosed with HIV. I knew she was hurting over Meagan's pregnancy, but her decision to drop out of school because of it affected Brittany personally.

Brittany looked at me. "Laurel, I'm sorry I ruined your relationship with Branson. I know you really loved him."

I shook my head. "I forgave you for that a long time ago. Besides, it wasn't entirely your fault."

I had been crushed when she and Branson got intimate back in high school. Now, even though Branson and I attended the same college, we rarely saw each other and I was perfectly fine with that.

"But what I did was wrong," Brittany said.

"Yes, it was," I said. "But we all make mistakes. And I'm totally over it."

"I'm so glad," she said.

"Don't worry about it anymore, OK?" I said. "We just need to pray for each other." I looked back and forth between her and Meagan. "We're gonna be on different roads this year, but God is still going to connect us in spirit. The same Holy Spirit is in each of us. Every time we think of the Lord, who can see us in all places, we'll be together through Him."

Brittany sniffled. "It's still going to be an adjustment."

Reaching for her hand, I said, "Yeah, it will. But it won't be impossible, because the Word says, 'With God all things are possible.'"

Brittany squeezed my hand. Meagan smiled.

Brittany paid the bill and we left the restaurant full—not only with food, but with friendships that would last a lifetime. Though absent from one another in body, we would be together in our hearts.

The next morning, as I lay in bed, I heard my dad's voice. "You've gotta get up, Laurel. We've loved having you visit, but I need to take you back to school."

"My bags are already packed," I mumbled through my pillow. "Luke carried them to the car last night. Besides," I said, pulling back the covers and sitting up straight, "I'm already dressed."

My dad chuckled and left.

I brushed my teeth and put on my sneakers, then went to the kitchen where Mom had fixed a bowl of oatmeal for me. I gobbled it down, sad about leaving my folks but eager to get back to my college life.

"No tears, Mom," I told her when I walked outside to get in the car.

My brothers were standing on the front porch. "You guys be good and take care of each other." I knew they wouldn't heed my advice. They always managed to get into some kind of trouble.

After saying good-bye thirty or forty times, I hopped into the passenger seat and my dad backed out of the driveway, tooting his horn.

My father played the song "Butterfly Kisses" by Bob Carlisle on the CD player. The sweet lyrics about a father-daughter relationship that changes as she grows from a baby to a woman brought tears to our eyes. In the song, when the girl is young, she gives her dad sweet kisses that he treasures as she grows up. Seeing pride in me beaming from my dad's eyes, I could tell he treasured me.

I remembered when my dad took me to my first day of kindergarten. I'd wanted to stay home with my younger brothers, but Dad assured me that God was going to be with me in my class, so I didn't have to fear.

And he was right. All day long that first day, God was with me, even when Sally Jane tried to bump me in line. The teacher caught her, and I just knew the Lord was watching over me.

I remembered telling her, "See, Sally Jane? You can't be mean to Laurel Shadrach because all the angels are watching over me."

"Nuh-uh," she replied.

"Uh-huh," I shot back. "My daddy told me so."

From then on Sally Jane was really nice to me.

I leaned over and gave my dad a kiss on the cheek. "I still like giving you butterfly kisses."

My dad rubbed his eyes and smiled. "You're going to be all right," he said. "This is going to be an even better semester than your first one because you know what to expect now. You're good friends with your roommate, which will really help. You understand how much studying is required to do well. And you're gonna make that gymnastics team too."

I hadn't told my parents how horrible I was doing in gymnastics. I knew I had to tell them soon because they were going to have to start shelling out some money for tuition if I didn't get the scholarship. But I couldn't bring myself to say anything. I hated the idea of letting them down.

Still, I knew God would make a way.

"You don't have to come inside," I told my dad when he pulled into the parking lot outside my dorm. "You can just put my bags on the curb."

"On the curb?" he said in a disappointed tone.

"I know you need to get back."

"I've got time," he said, pulling the keys out of the ignition. "Let me walk you in. I'm not gonna stay and cramp your style." He got out of the car and opened the trunk.

I got out, too, and smiled at him. "You're never cramping my style, Dad." I chuckled. "Good thing, too, since you're going to be back here in a few weeks."

He stared at me in confusion. "I am?"

"Yeah," I said with a grin. "My sorority needs a chaplain for our initiation ceremony, and I recommended you."

"That's sweet of you," he said, hauling my heavy suitcases out of the trunk. "But didn't you have your initiation last semester?"

I grabbed the lightest bag. "After that freshman was murdered and Anna tried to commit suicide, the sorority decided to put it off. So I'm still a pledge."

The minute we got into my dorm room, Payton gave me a big hug. I had really missed her. It felt nice to know she had missed me too.

As Dad started setting the suitcases on my bed, we heard loud, blaring music from the other side of the bathroom. I knew it was Jewels. She was a feisty, spoiled freshman. Beneath all her toughness, I knew she just wanted to be loved. But dealing with her wore me out. She was always pulling stupid stunts that made me wish our paths didn't have to cross. I asked God to fix my attitude toward her.

My dad went through the bathroom and knocked on Jewels's door. When she didn't answer, he barged right in. I stayed in my room, not wanting to interfere. As I started unpacking, I wondered what he was saying to her.

Any other time I probably would have been angry at my father for stepping into my life and making a mess of it. But I figured Jewels deserved whatever he was giving her. She never listened to me or Payton. She didn't even listen to Judy, the dorm director. I wondered if she'd listen to my dad.

Pretty soon the music volume came down and Dad came back. The pastoral look on his face told me he'd resolved the issue, at least temporarily. He prayed with Payton and me and then headed home.

After my dad left, Jewels came into our room. "Why did you put your dad up to coming down on me?" she complained.

"I didn't," I said. "He talked to you on his own."

Jewels poked her bottom lip out in a pout and stomped back to her room.

"Why was she playing her music so loud anyway?" I asked my roommate.

"She told me she was celebrating," Payton said. "Anna's not coming back."

I plopped onto my bed. "What?"

"Anna came by with her mom yesterday and cleared out all her stuff. She said she was planning to take a semester off to rethink life."

I closed my eyes and started praying for Anna. Then I prayed for Jewels, Payton, Brittany, Meagan, Robyn, and myself. We all needed Him. I knew He would come through for each of us.

———————————

At our next sorority meeting, the big sisters surprised us pledges by holding the belated initiation ceremony earlier than anticipated. All twenty-six of us said our vows to be eternally committed to the sorority, and we became full-fledged members of the organization.

I was disappointed that my dad hadn't been chosen to speak at the ceremony, but the president (Jewels's sister, Julie Anne) said she figured word would get out if they invited him, and she didn't want to spoil the surprise. I accepted the decision of my big sisters graciously. The most important thing was that I was finally, officially, an Alpha Gamma Delta.

When I got home from the ceremony, I found out that Judy, the dorm director, was considering candidates to take Anna's place as Jewels's roommate. I called Robyn right away. She had wanted to be closer to Payton and me, so I thought she might jump at the chance.

She was thrilled with the idea. She came to our dorm right away and met Judy, who signed her up on the spot.

Jewels wasn't in the room when Payton and I helped Robyn move her things in. That evening, when Payton and I were cleaning our own room, we heard the two of them arguing. Soon Jewels and Robyn stormed into our room and started yelling.

"We've got to switch roommates," Robyn said.

"That's right," Jewels said. She pointed at me. "You need to move in with me, and this . . . person . . . can take your place here." She scowled at Robyn.

"Let's talk about this," I suggested. "What's the problem?"

"I can't live with her," Jewels said. "We have nothing in common."

I felt like telling Jewels she didn't deserve to have a roommate she liked after the way she'd treated Anna, taunting her and making her feel insecure. But I figured Robyn was tough enough to handle Jewels.

I turned to Robyn. "How do you feel about this?"

"You know I don't care for most white girls," she said, "because of the way I was treated by those rude girls at my high school." She nodded toward her new roommate. "Well, Jewels fits the same profile: white and snotty."

"You guys are gonna have to get along," I said. "We have peace over here, and we don't want to change that."

"And there won't be any more rooms available till next semester," Payton added.

Robyn and Jewels looked disappointed. Payton and I gave our suite mates hugs, then they went through the bathroom to their room.

I grabbed the broom from my closet and started sweeping, but then noticed Payton rocking back and forth on her bed.

"What's wrong?" I asked.

"I miss my granddad. I know he's in a better place and all, but I want him here, with me and my grandmother. She's all alone now." Tears rippled down my friend's face. "I didn't know it was going to be this hard. My granddad and I didn't talk every day, but he kept our family strong, and now he's gone."

I sat beside her on the bed. "It's gonna be hard for you to live without that good man you love so much. But God can comfort you if you turn to Him." I put my arm around her shoulder. "We don't always understand God's ways. I don't know why He called your grandfather home. But I do know he's happy there, hanging out with Jesus."

Payton wiped her tears and smiled through her pain. "Thanks for letting me dump on you."

"Any time," I said. "That's what friends are for. I've got some things going on this semester that are pretty scary too. I know I'll need you. I'm glad we're roommates and we can keep reminding each other that God's got us."

Payton gave me a big hug.

"With God's help, we're gonna weather the storms in our lives. And that's OK because we're just trying to adapt."

being
totally dismissed

You're not going to make the gymnastics team," Coach Burrows told me in her office. "I'm sorry."

Hearing the Gym Dawgs head coach say that was like hearing that I had a deadly illness. As I watched my childhood dream die, I wanted to lash out and say, "Your team isn't going to be anything without me. I'm a Christian, and I know God would bless this team if you let me be on it."

But I couldn't say that.

I thought about pleading with the coach, but I couldn't bring myself to do that either. Summer Love was the only other candidate for the last position on the team, so I knew who had beaten me out. Though I didn't like Summer's attitude, I couldn't blame the coach for choosing her over me. She had proven herself to be the better athlete.

How was I going to tell my parents? They were depending on me getting a gymnastics scholarship. Without it, they couldn't afford to keep me at Georgia. Maybe I could transfer to Florida and go to school with Brittany.

"You're a fabulous gymnast," Coach Burrows said. "You push yourself harder than anybody else. I hope you won't give up on gymnastics entirely."

My body started to shiver. As tears brewed inside me, I tried to hold myself together. I didn't want the coach to see me fall apart.

I looked out the window and saw the other girls on the team watching and trying to listen in on our conversation.

Lord, help me be strong, I prayed.

"Laurel," the coach said, folding her arms, "if you'd like, you can stay on as one of the team managers. That way, you could still practice."

I nodded, unable to speak. Walking away from the gymnastics team would be tough. But hanging around every day watching what I was missing would be even harder.

Coach Burrows smiled. "Think about it. But I need to know by the end of this week. If you're not going to take the position, I have to find someone else."

I shuffled to the door, then turned. "I hate to ask this, Coach, but does a team manager get any scholarship money?"

"Of course," she said with a smile. "But not a full scholarship. It will cover tuition and fees, but not the dorm room or food."

I couldn't hold back the tears. She got up from her desk and handed me a tissue.

"Thanks," I said wiping my eyes. "I'll get back to you with an answer real soon."

When I walked out of her office to get my stuff from the locker room, I heard cold, ugly remarks being whispered behind my back.

"Did she really think she was going to make the team?" one girl said.

"She'd better get some muscles on those arms," another said. "Team managers have to carry a lot of luggage."

So they had heard our conversation through the door.

"I hope she doesn't become a manager," I heard Summer say. "She should just walk away graciously."

"You guys are so shallow," said Shae, a senior with long red hair.

I turned around. All three of the girls who'd made rude comments about me were freshman.

Shae came up to me. "I'm sorry you didn't make the team. I know some of us didn't treat you very nice, but we do that to all freshmen."

"Thanks," I said, trying to hide my whirling emotions. Then I continued on to the locker room to get my stuff.

Nadia walked in as I started unpacking my locker. She was about five-foot-one and lived in my dorm. She had competed in the nationals and the Olympics. I'd envied her for years, but after we met in the gym, she had helped me practice and we'd become close friends.

She hugged me. "Some of the girls told me the bad news. I'm so sorry."

"Me too," I said, hugging her back.

"You've got to stay, Laurel," she said as tears flowed from our eyes. "I can't do this without you."

"Please don't try to convince me to stick around. I really believe God has something else for me."

Nadia took a towel from the showers and wiped her tears. "I'm sure He does. I'm just sad that you won't be here." Nadia dried my tears with her towel. "Can I walk back to the dorm with you?"

"Practice is about to start. I don't want you to get in trouble over me."

"I'm sure Coach won't mind," she said.

I smiled. "I'm OK. Really."

As we embraced again, the assistant coach called practice to start. Everyone began walking toward the middle of the gym floor. I said good-bye to Nadia and left.

Being part of that team was something I'd wanted for a

long time. I held on to the assurance that God had to have another plan for me. But even with that hope, my anxiety level was high.

I started back toward my dorm room, hoping no one would be there. I was so fragile, I felt that if someone just said hello, I might have a panic attack.

It was raining hard. I had an umbrella, but I didn't open it. I just let the rain pelt me. It felt as if God was cleansing the whole gymnastics thing from my system.

Halfway to my dorm, Summer came up behind me. "Are you nutty?" she said as she held an extra-large yellow umbrella over both of our heads.

I kept walking, my hands stretched up to the sky, wanting God to rain down on me and fill me with His Spirit.

Summer kept up with me, hunkered under her umbrella. "Coach ended practice early because of the weather. Said we'd better get home before we get trapped in the gym."

I really didn't want her invading my space when I was obviously messed up. So I jogged away without a word.

––––––––––––

The next day I attended a sorority meeting, but my heart wasn't in it. Every recommendation I made, Jewels challenged. I said we could visit the elderly; she wanted to pick up trash on the streets. I knew her suggestion didn't have anything to do with performing a good deed. She just wanted people to see her on the side of the road.

However, the girls listened to her and she won out. Before I could object, she cut me off. I threw my hands up and stormed out of the meeting.

I ran to the bathroom upstairs, but several of the older sisters were in there so I started to leave. When I turned around, there stood Jewels with a smug look on her face.

"What do you want?" I asked. "If you're going to tell me I shouldn't be upset that you're trying to take over the meeting, forget it." I rattled off a bunch of other harsh words, coming down pretty hard on her.

To my surprise, she stood in the bathroom doorway and took it.

When I ran out of cutting things to say, she said quietly, "You told me this sorority wasn't about me, but about all of us. Well, you should take your own advice."

I stood there speechless.

"When I went home over Christmas break," she said, "I took a good look at myself. I realized I've always insisted on having things my own way, and I decided to change that."

Jewels looked sincere as she eyed me face-to-face. I was unimpressed. But I let her plead her case.

"Now you're acting like that. Your ideas aren't bad, but neither are mine. For some strange reason, the girls are choosing my suggestions for a change, and now you're all jealous. You need to get over it, Laurel. We're sisters. I'm not trying to hurt you. And I don't want your job as pledge class president."

I walked away and sat on the first hallway bench I could find. The sun beamed brightly in my face through a window. Was I acting like a jerk because I was still mad about not making the gymnastics team? I sighed.

Suddenly I heard my dad say, "Why don't you go back into the meeting, honey?"

I looked up and saw my father standing in the hallway. "Dad!"

He reached out his hand to help me up from the seat.

I stood and hugged him. "What are you doing here?"

As we pulled apart he said, "I'm praying for your sorority today."

"Cool," I said.

"Your friend is right, you know."

I looked at Jewels, who had followed me down the hall. She smiled at me.

"The sorority is not about an individual," he said. "It's about sisterhood."

"Yeah, I know," I said. "Thanks, Dad." I hugged him again, then shared an embrace with Jewels.

The three of us walked into the meeting room together. My father prayed with us. Then he talked to us for a while, blessed us, and left.

Later that evening Payton, Robyn, and I were watching a silly comedy on TV. I was lying on my bed, and Robyn was sitting beside me. Payton sat on her bed beside the desk. The two of them were laughing hysterically, and for some reason it irritated me.

"Enough already," I said. "It's not that funny."

"What's your problem?" Robyn asked.

"This isn't even your room," I grumbled, still stressing about my gymnastics failure.

Payton gave me a strange look. "Robyn is my guest, too, and if you don't want her on your bed, she can sit over here with me."

Robyn joined Payton on her bed. "What's up with her?"

"Give her a break," Payton said. "Obviously something's going on."

I got up and went to the bathroom.

After a few minutes Payton knocked on the door. "Do you want to talk?"

"No." I washed my hands, dried them off, then came out of the bathroom and sank onto my bed.

Payton looked at me with sad eyes. "When you want to talk, you know where to find me. You were there for me when I was upset about my granddad. I'm not going to bail on you."

"Thanks," I said. "It's nice to know you'll be there when I'm ready."

Tears flowed as she hugged me. Then we went back to watching the movie.

Sitting there with friends who accepted me made my pain, anger, and anguish easier to deal with. Everything was going to be OK. God would give me a vision for what was next for me. The door had shut on gymnastics, but I knew He would open a window somewhere.

"Hello? Is anybody there?" asked an irritated male voice on my phone.

I had called Foster, my other ex-boyfriend from high school. He had been a strong Christian friend, even after we broke up, and I knew he could give me a word of advice to help me out of my sadness. I hadn't really thought about what I was going to say to him, and after I dialed his number, I almost hung up. When he said hello, I knew I had to say something. So I said, "It's me. Laurel."

"Is everything OK?" Foster asked.

I told him about not making the gymnastics team.

"All right," he said, "so one dream seems like it's not going to happen right now. But that's OK. Hold on to your hope. Hold on to your passion. Hold on to your faith. The Laurel Shadrach I knew had ankle injuries and other setbacks, but she didn't let any of that bother her. Maybe you'll make the team next year."

"But this is the big leagues," I argued. "It's not easy."

"I know. I'm on a college team too. You just have to be strong. Count on the Lord."

"I'll try," I said.

"Let me pray with you." He poured out his heart to God and asked the Lord to take care of my soul.

"Thanks for being a great friend," I said after he said amen. "I miss this."

"Me too. Don't ever feel like you can't call me. We've got a special bond. I'm always here for you. And God is too. So be encouraged."

The next day, the air was cold and the ground icy. When I got to the library, it was more packed than usual. I went immediately to the third floor, but I didn't see Charlie. Instead a crowd of people were hovering around my favorite table, chatting.

"Excuse me," I said, "but do you mind if I sit here?"

One nerdy guy looked up and snapped, "We're talking."

"Can't you continue your conversation elsewhere?" I suggested. "I'd like to actually use the table for studying, not just stand around it."

He and his friends laughed. But their laughter died suddenly when they saw something over my shoulder.

As they backed away from the table, I turned around. My eyes lit up when I saw Charlie. He was just over six feet tall, had a cleft in his chin, and wore his brown hair short on the sides and curly on top, with streaks of blond.

I gave him a big hug, then realized I was showing too much of a public display of affection, so I backed off.

"You didn't have to stop," he said. "I've been looking for you all over the place." He grabbed my hand. "I haven't seen you in a couple of days."

As I looked at him, I started to cry, and he pulled me close to him. Then we sat at our table. "What's wrong?" he asked.

"I didn't make the gymnastics team," I blurted out.

"It's their loss," he said, wiping a tear from my cheek.

His words gave me the strength to smile. "Thanks."

"Want to talk about it?"

"Not really," I said.

He nodded, and we both began to study.

As we walked back to my dorm that night, he asked, "You OK?"

"I'll be fine," I told him with a smile. And I was. God was showing me there was more to life than gymnastics.

When I got back to the dorm, I decided it was time to explain to Payton what I was going through and to apologize for the way I'd been behaving. But when I walked into the room, she asked, "Can we talk?"

"Sure." I put my backpack on the floor.

"I know why you've been on edge," she said. "I heard you didn't make the team."

"That has been bothering me. But I'm OK now."

"I'm glad. Something better will come along. Don't worry."

I was so blessed. I had a loving family, good friends, and a heavenly Father who cared. I was no longer upset about being totally dismissed.

f i v e

standing
really tall

Several days had passed since I'd seen Charlie at the library. For some reason it was killing me. But that night we'd agreed to meet each other. I twirled around my room as if I were dancing with an invisible man.

I went to the bathroom and splashed water on my face to cool myself down. When I looked in the mirror, I imagined Charlie's perfect smile flashing back at me.

Get a grip, I told myself. *He's just a guy. You don't even really know him.*

I went into my bedroom, opened my window, and stuck my head out, letting the cold winter breeze blow on my face.

I wondered where Payton was. I needed to talk to someone. I called Nadia.

"Help me," I said when I heard the phone being answered.

"Who is this?" a girl's voice said.

"I'm sorry. May I talk to Nadia?"

"She's not here."

I punched my pillow. "I really need to talk to her."

"Wait," the girl said. "She's coming in now."

"Hello," Nadia said.

"I'm so glad you're there," I said.

"I wondered when it was going to hit you. I'm sorry you didn't make the squad."

"That's not the problem. Do you remember me telling you about the guy I met in the library?"

"Yeah, vaguely."

"I've been around him for a while, but I don't even know his real name."

"That's weird," she said.

"Yeah, it is," I said, "but I kind of like it. The mystery keeps things interesting."

We talked for about twenty minutes, and she basically told me what I already knew. I couldn't lose focus. I had to follow God. Hearing her say it out loud made me feel stronger.

"Keep taking it to God in prayer," she suggested. "You've got to give your relationships to God. He brought this guy into your life . . . at least He allowed you to meet him. Your feelings for him are getting deep. Just trust God to guard your heart."

"You're right."

Just then my phone beeped. I checked the caller ID and recognized the number. "I gotta go. That's my grandmother. I hope everything's OK with my grandfather."

"Me too," Nadia said.

"Thanks." I clicked to the other call. "Hello, Grandma."

"Why haven't I heard from you lately?" my grandfather said in his fake "tough voice."

I stood. "Granddad!"

"Oh, don't act like you're happy to hear my voice."

"But I am," I said.

"Did you think the old battle-ax was calling to tell you I'd kicked over?"

"Don't talk like that," I said.

"Why not? You're in college. I can be myself around you now. So, how are you handling those southern boys?"

"Don't worry," I told him. "I can take care of myself."

I wanted to ask Granddad if he had accepted the Lord yet. But before I could bring up the subject, he said, "Get out a pen and paper."

I reached into the drawer next to my bed and pulled out a notepad and ballpoint.

"This is important, so I want you to write it down. Are you ready?"

"Yes, Granddad," I said, pen poised.

"Men like strong women."

"Excuse me?" I said.

"We kinda like it when you sound a little dense now and then, but we want it to be an act. Smart wins out every time, particularly in this day and age. So get some knowledge from that dumb Georgia school you're going to."

I laughed. Granddad had wanted me to go to the University of Arkansas, his alma mater.

I wrote on my paper, *1. Self-assurance.* "What else?"

"Have your own life. Be secure in who you are. No man needs a woman who nags."

I wrote, *2. Confidence.*

"And always look good."

"What?" I asked.

"Be a fox, a knockout, as gorgeous as you can be. No matter what a man says, he wants a girl who's so pretty other people are always looking at her. Even if you're having a bad day, try not to show it."

3. Appearance.

"Know his likes and dislikes. And teach him yours as well."

4. Communication.

"You follow my advice and you'll have your pick of the litter."

"Yes, sir," I said, staring at my list, not sure I agreed totally with him, but happy he'd shared his wisdom with me. "Now, how are you doing?" I asked.

"Oh, I'm fine."

Before I could say "Good-bye," "I love you," or "Have you given your life to Christ?" he hung up.

I put the notepad in my desk and lay down on the bed. My pillow had never felt softer.

———————————

In the basement of the Alpha Gamma Delta house, eighty chairs were set up auditorium style. All the new members were seated toward the back, with the upper-class sisters in front of us. The six officers—the president, vice president, treasurer, financial secretary, corresponding secretary, and recording secretary—were on the dais ready to conduct the meeting.

I tried to pay attention when Julie Anne, the president, began giving her report, but I wasn't very interested in the things they were discussing. I knew I needed to do everything as unto the Lord, even if it wasn't stuff I had come up with. I had to learn to follow as well as lead. But my emotions were having trouble taking the backseat.

"You're lying, Jewels," a girl in the row behind me said loudly. "I know you said something about me."

I turned around and saw that the complainer was a girl from my dorm named Jill. She had light skin and short hair. I had walked to several meetings with her and her roommate, Mandelyn, before the weather got cold and I started riding with Jewels.

"What's wrong?" I asked.

Julie Anne told us to keep it down, so we all turned our attention to the podium. When she resumed her report, I turned around to check on Jill.

The veins in the girl's neck bulged as she leaned forward in her seat. "That suite mate of yours has ruined my reputation," she whispered.

"I did not," Jewels responded, casually blowing on her freshly polished nails.

Robyn kept her eyes forward, but her leg was shaking.

"It seems one of our freshmen sisters has something she wants to say," Julie Anne remarked.

Jill stood, drew back her fist, and threw a punch towards Jewels's face. Jewels got up and lunged toward Jill. I pulled the two of them apart before Jewels could swing back.

"What's going on back there?" Julie Anne asked from the podium.

"Everything's fine," I said, escorting Jill and Jewels to a quiet room down the hall.

I closed the door. "You guys need to talk."

"Forget it," Jill lashed out, flicking her hand at Jewels, who was standing nonchalantly in a corner.

"Jill, you have to calm down."

"Why should I?" Jill protested. "You're gonna take her side anyway."

"I am going to be completely impartial," I assured her. Then I strolled over to Jewels's corner of the room.

"I think I understand what's going on with you," I said quietly.

"Oh, you do, huh?" Jewels said arrogantly, rolling her eyes.

"You're jealous. You're mad that people don't like you as much as they like your sister, and Jill's getting pretty popular too. I know that hurts."

She folded her arms and looked away.

"You need to deal with what's going on with you without taking it out on other people. So what if Jill's popular today? Tomorrow it might be you, but not if you keep alienating people."

Jewels fixed her gaze on me. "I wanted to be pledge class president, but you got the job. Then I wanted to be project director, but everyone voted for Jill."

"So let's all talk about this," I suggested.

Jewels took a deep breath. "All right," she said sullenly.

I nodded for Jill to come sit with us, which she did. When I took a seat, making a small circle, I said, "Jill, why don't you tell us what your grievance is."

Jill looked at me. "I showed up at the fraternity house the other day to do some studying with my friend Tim," she said. "He kept looking at me weird. I finally asked him what his problem was. He said there's a rumor going around about me and that Jewels started it."

"What kind of rumor?" I asked.

"That I'm loose, that I'll get with anybody."

We both looked at Jewels.

"OK," Jewels said, "I did talk to Tim. He's in my trigonometry class, and he asked me if I knew you. He said he kinda likes you, but he heard you're a little wild."

"So you confirmed that I was?" Jill shrieked.

"No," Jewels said. "But I didn't deny it either."

"Why not?" Jill demanded.

"Hey, I don't know you. I see you around the dorm and at sorority meetings, but that's all."

"We're sorority sisters," Jill said. "You should have defended me."

"If it's not true, who cares what other people think?" Jewels said with a shrug.

"You care what other people think," I pointed out to her.

Jewels dropped her head.

"Why didn't you defend Jill?" I asked.

Jewels folded her arms.

"OK, I'll tell her." I turned to Jill. "Jewels is going through a difficult time right now."

I explained to Jill how Jewels felt about missing out on

the positions she'd wanted. As I spoke, I saw Jill's eyes turn from harsh to compassionate.

"I totally understand," Jill told Jewels. "I have an older sister too. She goes to the University of Alabama, so we don't have any issues now. But when we were in high school, I couldn't stand her."

"I know what you mean," Jewels said.

Jill stood and gave Jewels a big hug. They both apologized to each other. Then they started talking, and I was amazed at how they connected. They even started laughing and joking.

I thanked the Lord for allowing me to stand in the gap for Him and be the bridge that joined these two girls. Getting them together sure felt good.

When I walked to the table in the library where I always sat, my heart skipped three beats. It seemed like an eternity since I'd seen Charlie, even though it had only been a few days. Before that moment I'd had a handle on my feelings. I had set my priorities: God, self, family, school. But when I saw his face, Charlie was the only thing that mattered.

Lord, help.

I watched him talking to three guys at the table. One had curly hair, another had spiky hair, and the other had long brown hair. I'd first encountered this group last semester when I was trying to study at the library. Though I couldn't hear what they were saying to Charlie, I could tell my guy was winning the debate.

He looked up as I got near and smiled at me. "Hi, there."

Had he missed me like I'd missed him? I doubted it. He probably just wanted me to be on his side of the argument.

"What's going on?" I asked, taking a seat beside Charlie.

He whispered in my ear, "I'll be right back. I need to talk to these guys for a minute." He took them to a corner and spoke quietly but intensely.

"Oh," I heard Danny say, "she doesn't know?"

I walked up to the group. "Know what?"

Danny held his hand up. "Just go back to your seat, little Miss Georgia."

All the guys except Charlie laughed. But Charlie nodded his agreement.

Was the name he'd called me a compliment? It didn't sound like one. Then again, maybe I was just being paranoid. I walked back to the table and sat down again. I opened my books and studied, occasionally peeking at Charlie and trying to listen to what he was saying to the guys.

"Don't let her see the newspaper," I heard Danny say. I noticed him glance at a stack of stuff on the table next to mine. A local newspaper was stuck between two textbooks.

"Thanks a lot," Charlie said sarcastically.

The guys all gave Charlie a hand slap, then gathered their stuff and walked away. Charlie smiled as he sat back beside me.

"All right," I said, "what's going on?"

"We were just talking about the football team."

I peered at him curiously. Charlie had never seemed to care about football. "What about it?"

"There's a new coach."

"Are you serious?" I asked.

Charlie opened his backpack. "You say it like that's a bad thing."

"Well, it is. I hate for anybody to lose their job."

"He's a mean guy," Charlie said forcefully. "The new coach is a believer, and he's more concerned about making sure souls are saved than whether the team wins or loses."

"How do you know?" I asked.

Charlie searched in his backpack for something. "The guys were telling me." His forehead started sweating. "So, how are you?"

I sneezed. "I've got a cold coming on." I sneezed again.

"I need a tissue. I'll be right back." I got up and raced toward the restroom. I'd stuffed a travel pack of tissues into my purse before I left the dorm. But I needed an excuse to go find Danny and ask him and his friends what they had been talking to Charlie about.

I glanced back at the table to make sure Charlie wasn't watching, then I took the elevator down to the first floor. After glancing down all the aisles, I scooted out the main door. I looked in all directions but couldn't see the guys anywhere. With a sigh, I went back into the library and took the elevator back to the third floor.

As I approached our table, I stopped dead in my tracks. Three girls were handing Charlie slips of paper and pens. He was smiling, laughing, and writing something on the papers—his phone number, I presumed. I recognized the giggling girls as Chi Omegas: sassy, smart, and sexy. I stood there watching them, waiting for Charlie to shoo them off. But he never did. My hands got sweaty. I stepped a little closer, out of Charlie's line of vision but close enough to catch some of the conversation.

One of the girls started asking him about football. I couldn't imagine why. He was more of a bookworm than a sports fan. Almost a nerd, actually. Cute, but definitely not an athlete. Maybe the manager type, but he would have mentioned that to me by now.

When he looked up and saw me standing there, he ended his conversation quickly, like he'd gotten caught doing something wrong. He told the girls good-bye and came over to me.

"How much of that did you hear?" Charlie asked as I walked to the table.

"Why does everyone think you're a sports expert?"

"Beats me. You have a problem with it?"

"Yeah," I said. "I told you I'd never date another football player."

"Surely they aren't all bad," Charlie said, grinning.

"No," I said, "just not good enough for me to date."

He stared at me in silence. I suddenly realized he might have been thinking of trying out for the team, and I was basically telling him we had no future if he did.

We sat down and studied in silence. I did my math homework and he studied for a history test.

"Are you interested in one of those girls?" I asked, breaking the silence.

"Why would you ask that?"

"I saw you give them your phone number."

He grinned. "You saw me writing, but it wasn't my phone number."

"Oh, I suppose it was a homework assignment."

Charlie looked at me. "I like girls that are into sports. Much more than the prissy sorority kind."

A lump went into my throat. I hadn't told Charlie I was in a sorority. Though we'd been talking for weeks, our conversations had focused on studies, gymnastics, and God.

I got up and started to walk away. Charlie caught up to me and blocked my path. He stared at me. I didn't know if he was going to kiss me or tell me he never wanted to see me again. He was standing really tall.

feeling
really special

the way Charlie looked at me as we sat at our table in the library made me feel beautiful, perfect, and together. He didn't touch me or say a word, but his eyes spoke volumes. I felt more connected to him than I'd ever felt to any guy.

He saw my faults and accepted them. He saw my strengths and applauded me for them. He saw my weaknesses and was praying for them. He saw my joy and was happy for me. He saw my beauty and appreciated it.

But Charlie had said he wasn't into sorority girls. Would I lose my special connection with him if he found out I was one?

"So," he asked, "are you jealous?"

I heard giggles behind me. Those cute Chi Omega girls were looking at us. A tingle went up my back.

"Yes, I am," I admitted.

I opened my book and stared at the page. I felt proud of

myself for admitting my feelings. But now that I'd come clean, the ball was in his court.

I figured he wouldn't have asked me that question if he didn't want me to respond in the affirmative. But he probably hadn't thought I'd admit it.

After a few minutes, Charlie asked, "How often do you come to this library?"

His question confused me. We'd been meeting at the library for weeks, although he wasn't always there at the same time I was. "I usually come in here four or five nights a week."

"But I'm only here twice a week. Who do you talk to when I'm not here? Do you have another Charlie?"

I looked him in the eye. "What if I did?" I taunted.

He grabbed my hand. "I'd be jealous."

I felt myself blushing. I pulled back my hand, then instantly wished I'd left it in his. "So, where do we go from here?"

"We give our relationship back to the One who brought us together," he said. "Can I pray for us?"

I closed my eyes and bowed my head.

He clasped both of my hands in his. "Lord," he said, "thank You for allowing me to voice some of my feelings for this beautiful lady. Thank You for allowing the affection I have for her to be reciprocated." He squeezed my hand. "We're both a little confused right now because we don't really know what to do or which way to take these feelings. So we ask You to guide us and to make our relationship whatever You want it to be."

"God," I prayed when he paused, "let us feel You leading us. Give us Your strength, Your wisdom, and Your love. As I hold this precious hand in mind, I thank You for our friendship and for the next level we want to take it to. In Your Son's holy name. Amen."

"Amen," he said.

When I opened my eyes, I saw Charlie smiling at me. I

wanted God's best for him, and I was ready to embrace whatever was next for us.

"Can we get together next Saturday and go for pizza?" he asked.

"That'd be great."

I couldn't wait until Saturday for the Lord to reveal a little of His plan. I felt a sense of priority in this relationship. It was God first and us second.

That night I woke up several times. It was Friday, so I didn't have to get up early the next morning. I could just sleep in and be lazy.

Before I was ready to get up, the phone rang. I picked it up quickly before it woke Payton.

"Sorry to wake you," a girl's voice said. "I was just wondering if I could treat you to breakfast."

I looked at the clock. It was 6:40. "Who is this?"

"It's me, Nadia."

"What's going on?" I asked.

"I was planning to go work out, and I wondered if you could meet me in the cafeteria for breakfast."

"Is seven-thirty OK?" I asked, my mind starting to clear.

"I'll be there," she said.

My body was crying out for more sleep, but my friend had sounded like she needed me, and I wanted to be there for her.

I got dressed quietly, trying not to wake Payton. I hummed silently, thinking about Charlie's soft strokes across my face and his eyes shouting, "I care." The way he'd talked to God about us made me smile. Charlie wasn't the first guy who'd ever led me in prayer. My second high school boyfriend, Foster McDowell, was an absolute saint . . . practically an angel. But because of that, I never felt that he could really understand my struggles. With Charlie, I was beginning to understand and appreciate myself.

As I brushed my teeth, I wondered how I would make it through the hours before our date. His spirit made my heart flutter. Yeah, he was physically gorgeous. Even cuter than Branson. But Charlie's personality was even more charming.

When Nadia and I met in the cafeteria, there were at least fifteen people in line for food, which really surprised me for so early in the morning. When it was our turn to order, I got pancakes and sausage, and she chose a toasted raisin bagel with cream cheese. We found a table in the corner that was fairly secluded so we could talk privately.

Nadia's face looked sad.

"What's wrong?" I asked after taking a sip of orange juice.

"Stress," she said as she put her head in her hands.

"I'm sorry I missed the first couple of meets. I wanted to be there to support you, but some major things have been going on in my life."

"It's not that. I've actually been exceeding the coach's expectations. I moved up in the rotation and I'm already over a couple of seniors."

"That's great," I said as I rubbed her arm.

"I guess." She massaged her temples. "But I don't have any friends. No one who really cares about me. I've tried making small talk with the other girls on the team, but they just ignore me. They snicker when I make mistakes in my routine. And in the locker room, they talk about my performance like I'm not even there." She nibbled on her bagel. "I want to quit."

I practically spit out my bite of pancake. After swallowing my food, I said, "Does the coach know how you feel?"

"No. But telling her won't help. The other girls will isolate me even more if I say anything about the way they're treating me. Besides, I want real friends, not forced ones."

"I'm your friend," I assured her.

She looked up at me. "Thanks." She took a bite of her bagel. "So, what have you been up to?"

71

"Not much," I said. But thinking about Charlie painted a smile on my face.

"You met a guy, didn't you?" she guessed.

I chuckled. "Yeah."

"Tell me everything. What's his name? Where is he from? Does he have a brother?"

I ate my last bite of sausage, wiped my mouth, then told her everything I knew about Charlie. Nadia told me over and over how excited she was for me.

She put her arm around me. "I've been praying for you. Sounds like Charlie is an answer to prayer."

"He is pretty cool," I said with a smile.

As we walked out of the cafeteria, she told me our breakfast get-together had been just what she needed. "When you didn't make the team, I cried," she said.

I stopped dead in my tracks. "You did? That's so sweet."

"I was crying for myself a little, too, because I knew what would happen." She looked away. "When the other girls stopped trying to get you off the team, they started in on me. I thought I was tough enough to take it. But deep down I knew I needed your help."

I felt her pain. Friendship meant being your sister's keeper, feeling her highs, lows, joys, pains, and laughter. I was glad I could be there for Nadia. "I won't miss another meet if I can possibly help it," I promised.

I really wanted to tell Payton about Charlie. But when I got back to the dorm room, she was gone. We hadn't talked much for the last several days. It seemed I was always asleep when she got home or she was asleep when I got there.

I studied hard all week so I could forget about school-work on the weekend. I wanted to give all my attention to my date with Charlie.

The connection between the two of us was deeper than physical appearance, but I remembered what Granddad had told me. Besides, I wanted Charlie to smile at me the way he had at those Chi Omega girls. So I decided to give myself a manicure.

I didn't know where we were going on our date. I'd wanted to ask, but he hadn't called me. I didn't want to seem pushy, so I didn't call him either. I didn't even know if he was coming to pick me up or if we were supposed to meet somewhere.

I suddenly got a sick feeling in my stomach. What if the sweet guy I knew from the library turned out to be a rapist or murderer? As bizarre as that seemed, that's what apparently happened to a girl from my dorm the previous semester. She'd gone out on a date and never came back.

I would definitely tell Robyn my plans, just in case, as soon as I found out what they were. Someone should know where I was going and who I was going with.

I pulled a cream-colored top off its hanger and held it in front of me, then checked it out in the mirror. Just then I heard Robyn singing in the bathroom.

"Hey," I hollered, "can you come in here when you get a sec?"

Robyn opened the door. "What have you been up to? I've been asking Payton about you, and she said you've been doing an awful lot of studying." Robyn leaned against my dresser. "Now, tell me the real deal. What's up with the library?"

I felt my cheeks turning red.

"Come on," Robyn commanded, snatching the cream top out of my hand. "Tell me everything."

After I gave her the rundown on Charlie, she said, "We've got to find you a nice outfit. And we have to do something about that hair. Girl, you used to look cute back in high school. Now you just blend in with the rest of these white folks."

"Oh, and I'm supposed to stand out like you, huh?" I replied, nodding at her bright orange outfit.

She browsed through my closet and selected a gray wool

skirt and a peach cashmere sweater. They really did look cute together.

Robyn teased me about calling a hair salon and setting up an emergency appointment for me. She even suggested I go to a tanning booth.

"That's what you white girls do, right?" she said. "Go sit under lights so you can look more like us?"

I laughed. I loved the way we could tease each other about everything, even race.

"Girl, go get some rays on yourself. Not too much, though, cause I don't want you getting cancer or nothing."

"Don't tell Payton about Charlie, OK?" I said.

"Why not?" she asked.

"After Branson and I broke up, she made it her personal mission to try to get me a date. We haven't talked about it in a while because I haven't seen her lately. But I don't want her to pressure me about this new guy, you know?"

"Yeah, she is a matchmaker," Robyn said. "Did you know one of her old boyfriends wants her back?"

"I hope it's the good one," I said.

"Yes, it's Tad. He told her he's going to break up with his girlfriend so he can go out with Payton again."

"That's great," I said, changing into the outfit Robyn had picked out for me. "What about you? How are you spending your Saturday night?"

"Payton has me involved in some recruiting activities for the football team."

"Is that what you want to do with your weekend?" I asked, admiring myself in the mirror.

"I like being around the athletes," she said, plopping down on my bed.

"Any athletes in particular?" I asked, sitting beside her.

"Last week I met this majorly cute football player. We were paired up to take out a recruit. The two of us really vibed." She got up and started pacing the room.

"You're not thinking of sleeping with him, are you?" I

asked, remembering her involvement with Jackson Reid in high school. She still suffered from the emotional scars of her abortion.

"No way," she assured me. But she didn't look me in the eye when she said it.

"Then why do you look so anxious about this?"

"The guy is Payton's ex," she blurted out.

"Tad?"

"No, the other one. I know you think Dakari's bad, but I'm not perfect myself, so who am I to judge? I don't know if he likes me or not. But I can't put him out of my mind."

"Have you prayed about this?" I asked.

"Not really," she said, holding up the blush-colored lipstick she thought I should wear.

"Robyn, you've gotta trust God to work this out. Move only where He wants you to go."

"You're right," she agreed. "Now, you won't tell Payton about me going out with her ex, will you?"

"No," I said. "And you're not going to tell her about my date either, right?"

"Deal!" She sat back on the bed. "Thanks for telling me, though. It's been really fun helping you pick out an outfit. I miss you, girl. Now, you have a great Valentine's date tonight, OK?"

I hadn't realized it was Valentine's Day. What a sweet surprise to have a date on that special night. After Robyn left, I got to my knees and prayed for a great evening.

I put on my boots and my leather jacket. I looked in the mirror and felt great.

When my phone rang, I jumped on it.

"Are you still up for going out with me?" Charlie asked.

"Sure am."

"I'm outside," he said. "Can't wait to see you."

I hurried to the parking lot and found Charlie standing beside his black BMW. He looked great in a navy blazer, black shoes, jeans, and a blue turtleneck.

I called Robyn on my cell phone and left a message with his license plate number, just in case something went wrong.

As he opened the passenger door for me, Charlie said, "You look beautiful."

At that moment I was feeling really special.

dreaming isn't bad

I looked down at my hands. They were wrinkled and old. My long hair was gray. My dear Charlie, handsome as ever, was seventy years old. We had three children, two boys and a girl, who had grown into godly adults and had their own children.

The charming man who had won my heart had played in the NFL for thirteen years and went to the Pro Bowl six of those years. He was even in the Hall of Fame. After the NFL he attended seminary and took over my father's church.

"Are you OK?" Charlie asked, holding the car door open for me.

We hadn't even gone out on our first date, and there I was envisioning our future.

After I hopped into the car, Charlie closed my door and slid into the driver's seat. His hands shook on the steering wheel. It was cute to see him nervous.

"These are for you," he said, reaching into the backseat and pulling up a large bouquet of beautiful pink roses.

I thanked him, and I breathed in their heady fragrance as Charlie drove to a seafood restaurant.

After we were seated at an isolated table by the window, Charlie told me I had to try his favorite dish: lobster. During our library studies I had let it slip that I had never eaten it.

"Should I order for both of us?" he asked.

"Sure," I said. "But what if I don't like it?"

"They'll take it back." He stroked my arm with his hand. "Trust me. I eat here all the time."

The waiter gave us first-class treatment. I felt like a queen. I could definitely get used to this.

Charlie asked me about my week. When I told him I had been longing for this date, his nervousness began to subside.

Shortly after we received our sodas and salads, a man and his young son came up to our table and asked Charlie for his autograph. As he signed their paper napkin, I realized how much I didn't know about this guy. And I didn't like it.

"Are you an athlete?" I blurted out after the father and son left.

"What?" Charlie asked, looking nervous again.

I grabbed a slice of the bread. "Why else would people want your autograph?"

"If I was an athlete, I wouldn't tell you," Charlie joked, cutting a piece of lettuce. "You don't like athletes, remember?"

I smiled. Surely, he couldn't be an athlete. *Could he?*

The waiter arrived with our dinners. The lobster looked peculiar, sitting inside that hard red shell. I wondered how I was supposed to eat it. But the aroma of it, along with the baked potato loaded with butter, sour cream, and chives, made my mouth water.

Charlie reached over and easily pulled the lobster meat

out of its shell with his fork. Then he fed me my first bite of his favorite food. He was right. I loved the taste.

"I really want to get right with God," Charlie said as he gazed into my eyes. "I'm not where I should be in my walk with Christ, and I want to do all that I can for Him."

Charlie told me he longed to find a soul mate who would love him for who he truly was, not for what others thought he was. I wondered what he meant by that. How did other people think of him, and how was that different from his real self? Would I ever truly know this guy? And if he ever did let me inside his heart, would I like what I found?

We talked about trivial things. I learned that his favorite color was dark blue because his first childhood teddy bear was that color.

When we got back to my dorm, Charlie hopped out of the car quickly and opened the passenger door. When I got out, he rested his arm on the top of the BMW so I couldn't get past him. He didn't kiss me. But the way he looked at me made me feel even more special than his lips could have.

"Where do we go from here?" he asked, breathing on my neck.

"Let's just take it one day at a time. Who knows? We might wake up fifty years from now still enjoying nights like this."

My room was empty when I got back from my date with Charlie, and so was my suite mates' room, so I had the bathroom all to myself. I took full advantage of the rare opportunity. As I relaxed in the tub, I thought about what Charlie had said about wanting someone who would love him for who he truly was. Who was he, really? In a way, it bothered me that I didn't know. But the mystery of not knowing gave our relationship added suspense and excitement that I really liked.

UGA's president had a son who was a freshman. None of my sorority sisters knew what he looked like because he was rarely seen in public. Maybe Charlie was him.

After soaking for about twenty minutes, I got out of the tub and headed for bed. Before I could doze off, Payton came in, full of smiles.

She told me all about her evening. I wanted to tell her about mine. But when she told me Tad had asked her to be his girlfriend again, I decided to wait on my news and just rejoice with her.

She sat on my bed. "He said he dumped the other girl he was seeing. I feel bad for her and all, but I love him."

I wrapped my arms around her and squeezed her tight. "Don't mess it up this time," I teased her. "You let him go once. Now you got another chance."

"You're right. I'm going to be a lot smarter this time."

Jewels woke me up early the next morning by barging in through the bathroom. "Why didn't you come to the party last night?" she whined.

I looked over at Payton's bed and saw that it was neatly made.

"Do you really want to know where I was?" I asked, sitting up in the bed.

"Sure," she said. "But first I've got to tell you about this guy I met." She stood over me, beaming. "He's a Kappa Alpha."

"Which one?" I asked.

"He's not from Georgia. He goes to South Carolina. He just came down for the party. Anyway, he asked me to dance, and we were together all night. It was unbelievable. When he left, he invited me to a big party they're having in a couple of weeks. You've got to come. Most of the sorority is going."

"To South Carolina? No way," I said.

"But you've got to. Please," she said with a pitiful look on her face.

I placed my hand on her shoulder. "All right. If I don't have too much studying to do."

She hugged me and offered to spend the day with me getting our nails done, shopping, getting a tan, and having dinner. Spending time with Jewels wasn't my idea of an exciting way to spend my Sunday, but I didn't have any other plans, so I agreed.

When I woke up a few days later, I saw Payton putting on lipstick. She was dressed in a fitted red turtleneck sweater, tight jeans, and black high-heeled boots.

"You look really cute," I said.

She looked at me through the mirror. "Thanks. I'm going to a basketball game with Tad."

"You don't sound too happy about it," I said, picking out my own clothes for the day.

"It's not just the two of us," she said, turning to face me. "Some friend of his is tagging along."

"Oh," I said, feeling her disappointment.

"What are you doing tonight?" she asked.

I walked over to the desk we shared. "I've got some studying to do."

"Studying?" she teased. "You should be a genius by now after all the time you've been spending at the library. You must have read all the books in the place already."

"Get out of here and go have fun on your date," I said, handing her the purse sitting on her bed.

She took the purse and left. I looked in the mirror at my tangled hair and sweat suit. It had been a week since my date with Charlie. He hadn't called, but I didn't want to read too much into that. I'd gone to the library a couple of times, but he hadn't been there. Just in case he showed up that day, I wanted to look presentable. So I shed the sweat suit and

81

put on a pair of jeans, a thick blue sweater, black hiking boots, and a black leather coat.

My heart sank when I saw our library table empty again. The students who normally sat at the table across from us were there, though.

Danny saw me coming. "You looking for—" he said before his buddy punched him in the arm. "Oh, that's right," he mumbled, rubbing his elbow.

Confused at the gesture I said, "I'm not looking for anyone." I took my usual seat at the empty table.

"Yeah, sure," Danny teased me.

As soon as I pulled out my textbook, Charlie came up behind me. I melted. But I didn't want him to see how hurt I was that he hadn't called. So I looked back at my book.

"Did I do something wrong?" Charlie asked, taking the seat beside me.

"No," I said, not looking up.

"You're bummed out that we haven't talked," he said, reading my mind. "I know this will sound like a line, but I really have been swamped."

When I didn't respond, he grabbed my hand. "I was thinking of you, though. And I came to the library a couple of times this week but you weren't here."

My eyes met his and I smiled. "I did the same thing," I admitted.

"I'm glad you're here now," he said. "I just left a basketball game. I was on a date."

My face turned suddenly hot. I couldn't believe he had the gall to say that.

"Oh, no, let me explain. My buddy asked me to go with him on his date so I could meet his girlfriend."

I laughed. "That's funny. My roommate was in a similar situation."

"Really?"

I nodded. "So, how'd it go? Did you like his girlfriend?"

"She was nice. But clearly she didn't want me there. I

started thinking about you when I saw the cheerleaders doing all those flips. Maybe you should try out. Since you're so good at gymnastics, you'd be a dynamite cheerleader."

I felt apprehensive about the idea at first, but then I started wondering if cheerleading might be considered a sport. If so, there might be a scholarship available.

"I had a dream about you last night," Charlie said.

"Really?"

He took my hand. "I dreamed we had another date, and it was even better than the first one."

It thrilled my heart to hear that he was thinking of me subconsciously. "Tell me about it."

"Nah, you don't want to hear it," he teased.

"Don't you hold out on me, mister," I teased back, playfully threatening to punch him if he didn't spill the beans.

"OK, OK." He laughed. "I dreamed we were in Paris." He looked embarrassed. "Pretty far out, huh?"

I grinned. "Well, keep on dreaming," I told him, giving him a thumbs-up, "because dreaming isn't bad."

being
a light

i t was still winter, but spring was drawing near. The second semester was flying by faster than a speed skater.

I had to start planning my schedule for sophomore year, and I wanted to consider my classes carefully. But I'd been so busy with schoolwork, I hadn't had time to think about anything else. It felt like I was back in high school, going straight from one class to another.

Charlie and I hadn't gone on any more dates because we were both too busy. So we made the library at 7:30 our date time. One evening, when I arrived at the entrance, I found him on a bench in the courtyard with candles, a blanket, and Chinese food. The romantic evening made me feel special.

Jewels had really been buttering me up because she wanted me to go to South Carolina with her for that Kappa Alpha party. She didn't need to, though. I fully intended to keep my word and go with her.

I had found a church home and was focusing on my relationship with the Lord. My prayer life was full. I was happy. But Payton thought I needed a boyfriend. When I told her I didn't, she said she had found the perfect Christian guy for me and she insisted on setting us up on a blind date.

I was sure I wouldn't like anybody she had in mind for me because I'd already found Charlie. Though he wasn't verbally pressing for our relationship to move closer, his actions suggested that we were already close. We still kept our real names anonymous, though, because we liked the intrigue of it.

"I'm thinking about trying out for cheerleading," I told Payton, trying to get her off the subject of setting me up.

"Really?" she asked.

"I know I can do the flips, but the dances and the cheers, I'm not so sure about."

Payton's eyes lit up. "I've been thinking about trying out too. I can do the dances, but not the flips."

"I could teach you how to flip," I told her, "if you'll teach me how to dance."

"It's a deal," she said. "Let's start right now."

We stood in the small space between our beds and I tried copying her movements. Payton taught me a simple dance routine in about twenty minutes. I wasn't great at it, but I felt confident that I could get better with practice.

After that, we put on our sweats so I could teach her a few tumbling exercises. She caught on to the basics pretty quickly, although her movements weren't very crisp.

"If we could mesh ourselves into one person, we'd be the perfect cheerleader," I said.

We had less than two months before cheerleading tryouts. We both felt doubtful about our chances, but we were determined to try.

After Payton showed me some more moves, we held hands and gave our desire to become cheerleaders to God. If He wanted it to happen, nothing could stop us. We prayed that we would stay in His will and keep frustration out of the equation.

The next day, Payton and I went to the gym to practice. We felt pretty nervous, but after praying, we could actually see ourselves on the squad. God could do that. He could make a way. He had sent me a roommate who knew Him. We had called on Him together and He was showing us the way.

Would we end up becoming cheerleaders? We honestly didn't know, but we knew it was going to be a fun journey traveling down that road together.

The next evening I went to the library for my 7:30 date with Charlie. I found him just inside the front doorway.

"Can I help you carry your books?" he asked with his arms outstretched.

"You don't have any?" I asked, giving him mine.

He shook his head.

"Well, if you don't have to study, why are you here?" I teased him.

He grinned. He didn't have to answer. I knew he had come just to see me. He wasn't going to miss our time together. Charlie was doing everything right in our relationship, and boy, did that make me feel good.

We sat at our usual spot. Danny and his crew were at the table next to us.

I told Charlie I was struggling with some of the cheerleading moves. He encouraged me not to give up, that my hard work would pay off.

"You can make the team," he said, "but not alone. You need God to be there with you." He held my hands and closed his eyes. "Father, we thank You for giving us a vision. Thank You for using our gifts and talents and giving us the desire to please You and serve You with what You've given us. I pray right now for Laurel. Lord, she wanted so badly to be on the gymnastics team here, but it didn't work out, and we believe that's because You're opening the door for something else. Show her how to make the cheerleading squad if that's Your will, Father. Help her not to be afraid. I thank You for allowing our friendship to grow and develop. She's a special lady and I'm blessed to know her. We love You and praise You. Amen."

Danny leaned over from the next table. "Hey, were you guys praying just now?" he asked sarcastically.

"Yeah," Charlie said. "So?"

He snorted. "You really believe in *God?*"

Charlie stood, and I stood behind him. "If you died tomorrow," Charlie asked Danny, "do you know where you would go?"

"Yeah," the cocky guy answered. "I'll be in a box covered with six feet of dirt. I suppose you think you'll go up to the sky and live forever?"

The guys around Danny started laughing. My heart broke at their ignorance. Getting a degree was what we had come to school to do. But accepting Christ was what God wanted us to do. Unfortunately, they didn't know that.

"That's exactly what we believe," Charlie said with conviction.

"Oh, really?" Danny retorted. "What makes you think you're good enough to go to heaven?"

Charlie smiled. "I'm not. That's what's so great. I know I'm a sinner, but I'm going to heaven anyway. All I have to do is call on Jesus' name."

"Whatever," Danny said, turning away. "You believe whatever you want."

"I believe God is real. Just as real as you or me."

"Oh, yeah?" Danny said, looking Charlie in the eye. "Well, I prayed to Him when I was ten years old. I prayed that my dad would stay with my mom. A couple of days later, Dad walked out the door with all his stuff and his new girlfriend."

"I understand," Charlie said softly. "The God you believed in let you down."

"No kidding. If He answers prayers, then why didn't He answer mine?"

"I don't know," Charlie admitted. "I can't explain why that happened, but it has nothing to do with your salvation. You'll be judged someday, just like me. And when God asks why you didn't believe in Him, are you going to say it was because He let your dad leave you?"

Danny's buddies started snickering. But I could tell Charlie was making his point because Danny scratched his head and peered at the ceiling as if he were contemplating the possibility that someone might be up there. Then he shook his head, grabbed his book bag, and said, "C'mon, guys, let's go." He strutted to the elevator, his friends following close behind.

Charlie and I watched them leave.

"You were good," I said.

"Thanks," he said, sitting down. "But that was just the beginning of my work with that guy."

"I bet you wanted him to accept Christ right then, huh?"

"Sure. But I understand that I'm just supposed to lift up God to people, and He'll do the rest."

"You're a light in darkness, Charlie. I'm proud of you." I threw my arms around him.

"Thanks for your support," he said into my ear.

"I didn't do anything."

"You were by my side. It made me feel brave enough not to back down."

I released Charlie reluctantly.

"You want me to walk you home?" he asked.

I nodded.

An hour later, as I was resting in my bed, I decided to call Charlie. I opened my spiral notebook and found his phone number on the front page. I dialed. After the first ring his gentle voice said, "Hello, beautiful."

"You don't even know who this is," I teased him.

"I've got caller ID. What's up?"

"I just wanted to tell you again how proud I am of you," I said, lying on my bed. "I was really impressed with the way you did what the Lord calls us all to do: trying to get people to know God. You inspired me to do more of that myself."

"When am I going to see you again?" Charlie asked. "Do you want to get together tomorrow?"

"Yeah."

"And the day after that?"

"Sure."

"How about the day after that?"

"OK." I laughed.

"Great. I'll see you tomorrow at 7:30 in the library."

"Good night," I told him with a smile.

His "good night" back to me sent me into a sweet slumber.

"Are you ready yet?" Jewels asked the following Saturday, banging on the bathroom door.

"Almost," I huffed as I opened the door.

"You're not even dressed," Jewels cried in a panic.

"Hey, if you're in such a hurry, I don't have to go at all."

"Sorry," she said. "But the caravan is going to be pulling out soon."

Our basketball team was playing the University of South Carolina Gamecocks that night, and lots of folks from Georgia were going. A bunch of sorority girls were driving up together.

Things had been going so great between Charlie and me, I'd really wanted to get out of this. But I figured this would be a perfect opportunity to let my light shine for Jesus. Besides, Charlie had said he was busy that night. He hadn't told me what he was doing and I didn't ask.

89

Payton had left earlier that evening for a big SGA event she was chairing. She was the director of minority recruitment for our school. Her job was to entice more African-Americans to attend the University of Georgia.

Jewels talked all the way to the car and all the way on the drive to Columbia, and I couldn't squeeze in anything about her salvation. When she started bragging about Kelly, this fraternity guy she was infatuated with, I finally got up the nerve to talk about Christ.

"OK, OK," I cut in. "I don't need all the details about what you can't wait to do with this guy. But I do want to share my heart if that's all right."

"Sure," Jewels said as she took her eye off the road for a second to glance at me.

"Please don't think I'm trying to throw stones. I know I'm not perfect." After taking a second to choose my words carefully, I said, "When we become Christians we shouldn't do the things we used to do. You know, like having sex."

As she came to a stop at a red light, she looked over at me. "Laurel, I'm a virgin."

I was dumbfounded and relieved at the same time. Because of her flirty ways, I had assumed she wasn't pure.

"That's great," I said, hiding my surprise. "You should stay that way until marriage."

"Why?" she asked, taking off when the light turned green.

"Because God said so."

Jewels shot a glare at me.

"Besides, we have way too many issues in college without worrying about sex too. If you have sexual relations with a guy, there could be emotional or physical fallout. I don't want to see you regret your decision. Trust me, Jewels. From my experience—"

"Your experience?" she asked with squinted eyes.

"Oh, I'm a virgin too," I clarified. "But my high school friends have gone through stuff. One had an abortion and has emotional scars from it. Another got a disease that she has to control by medicine or she'll die. And another is carrying a baby that she's going to give up for adoption, which is making her really sad." I put my hand on Jewels's arm. "I care about you. I just want you to be smart."

She sighed. "Well, I can't promise what I'll do tonight."

Closing my eyes, I quickly prayed for her. If she ran into a mess, I wanted to be there for her to help pick up the pieces.

When we drove onto fraternity row, all the cars around us started beeping their horns and people were hanging out of windows yelling, which made it impossible to discuss serious issues. So I decided to stop talking and just let my words take root in her heart, where the Holy Spirit could nurture them and make them grow in time.

When we got out of the car at the fraternity house, Jewels started looking for Kelly. She found him pretty quickly and introduced me, fawning all over him.

Before I could say anything more than "Hello," Kelly whisked Jewels away. I followed them upstairs, but when they went into a room, I decided to go back down to the living room with the rest of the people.

Everywhere I looked, college kids were making out. If I'd had Jewels's car keys, I would have gone back to Athens right then. Instead, I sat in a corner and watched the couples on the dance floor.

Forty minutes later, Jewels came downstairs, hand in hand with Kelly. He dragged her onto the dance floor, where he started thrusting his tongue down her throat.

A bunch of rowdy guys in the next room started chanting about a drinking contest. A few of them came up to Kelly and pulled him away from Jewels. When one of them slapped a mug of beer into his hand, Kelly started drinking and shouting with them.

Jewels's body swayed as she stood there watching Kelly. I grabbed her hand and led her to a relatively quiet corner.

"What happened, Jewels?" I asked.

She smiled. Then, to my horror, she told me she'd just lost her virginity.

"It felt so good," she said. "I'm a little sore, but Kelly said when we get together next time it'll be better."

I stared at her. I couldn't believe she was thinking of sleeping with this guy again when he obviously didn't respect her.

"Let's go watch the contest," she said. Without waiting for an answer, Jewels dragged me to the corner where Kelly and three other guys stood in front of some kegs of beer, trying to see who could drink the most.

After four rounds, only Kelly and one other guy were still drinking. Kelly's face turned red and then blue. Then suddenly he fell forward, hitting his head on the edge of a coffee table. Blood started pouring from his forehead.

Jewels rushed to his side. I knelt beside her. "He's not breathing," she screamed.

A USC girl wearing an Alpha Gamma Delta shirt shouted, "I'll call 9-1-1!"

I started performing CPR on Kelly. I was scared, but my instincts kicked in. I checked his airway, then listened to see if he was breathing. When there was no response, I gave him mouth-to-mouth resuscitation.

"Come on, baby," Jewels screamed. "I just found you. I don't want to lose you already."

People crowded around the limp body in front of me. "Save him," someone screamed.

Then I heard a familiar voice. "Step back, you guys; give her room." I looked up and saw Branson, looking as handsome as ever. "She's been CPR trained," he told everyone.

I went back to trying to save Kelly. But he wasn't responding. There was no pulse.

"He's gone," someone hollered.

"No," Jewels said. "Keep trying, Laurel!"

I knew I had to continue pumping this guy's chest until

help arrived. Even though I was mad at him for taking Jewels upstairs, I needed to put that aside.

After several minutes, I sat back, ready to give up. My arms were sore and Kelly simply wasn't responding to my efforts.

Jewels wrapped her arms around me. "He's going to be OK," she said. "You believe that, don't you?"

I didn't know what to say.

"Come on, Laurel, I need you. Don't quit on me now. Don't stop being a light."

N I N e

accepting
God's will

i kept pumping Kelly's chest, but no response came from the body that lay before me. I had to keep going. I couldn't stop. Any second he could come to.

The crowd around me drew in closer. I felt hot all over. Sweat dropped from my chin onto my shirt. I felt like I couldn't breathe.

"Get back," I screamed. "I need room!"

I pounded the guy's chest with my fists. Then I felt a gentle touch on my shoulder and heard a soft male voice say, "That's enough."

Branson knelt beside me and took my hands. Then he pulled me to him and held me close.

"I don't want his life to be over," I moaned.

Branson gave me a small smile. "Laurel, the paramedics are here."

I turned and saw three paramedics. When I pulled back,

they knelt beside Kelly's body, checked his pulse, and started performing CPR.

As I looked on, I became paralyzed with the shock of watching someone die before my eyes.

Four police officers cleared most of the kids out of the room. Branson and I, Jewels, and a few of the fraternity guys were allowed to stay. Brian, the fraternity president, told the police what happened. Jewels held Kelly's hand and stared at his lifeless body. I collapsed into Branson's arms, praying that I would wake up from this nightmare.

The paramedics continued performing CPR and gave Kelly drugs to stimulate his heart. Finally they gave up.

"No," Jewels wailed as the paramedics lifted her boyfriend's body onto the stretcher and covered it with a thick white cloth.

Sobs, screams, and cries filled the air. My body started trembling. I couldn't believe this life that I had worked so hard to save was gone. I broke away from Branson as the paramedics wheeled Kelly's body down to the ambulance. They put him in the back and drove off. My body felt cold.

Jewels flew into Branson's arms and they cried together.

Lord, I cried, *why didn't You save him?*

Then a thought hit me. Had Kelly accepted Jesus Christ before he died? Was he on his way to heaven?

I started asking all the people around me if Kelly knew Jesus. They all looked at me like I was crazy, but I didn't care. I just kept asking. Unfortunately, no one knew the answer.

I heard two policemen talking to each other, and one of them said Kelly's parents were going to meet the ambulance at the hospital. "I didn't tell them their son was already dead," he added quietly.

I walked over to Branson, who was talking with some of the fraternity members. "I need to go to the hospital."

"Me too," Jewels said, grabbing my hand and squeezing it.

"I'll drive," Branson offered. We hopped into his blue Camaro. A few other guys in the fraternity followed in another car.

We all congregated in the waiting area of the emergency room. A few moments later, a man and woman in their midforties came from behind a curtain. They looked as if their world had been completely shattered. Tears streamed down their faces. The woman chanted, "How can Kelly be gone? How can my baby be gone?"

Jewels fled to the lady, and the two of them embraced.

Branson came up beside me. "Are you OK?"

I fell into his arms. "I tried my best to save him," I choked out between sobs. "I can't believe he died right in front of me."

"You did all you could."

"I wish I knew if Kelly accepted Jesus Christ before he died." I had never witnessed to the guy. Would he be with the Savior when he woke up? My heart broke that this young man's life was over, but I was shattered at the thought that he might not spend eternity in heaven.

Branson fell into the nearest chair and put his hands to his face.

Jewels told Kelly's parents what I'd done for him. They thanked me over and over for trying to save their son.

"I know you did your best," his father said as he shook my hand. "It was just our son's time."

"Was Kelly a Christian?" I asked.

His mom's knees collapsed. Her husband caught and held her.

"We don't know," Kelly's dad said in a hoarse voice. "We pray he was."

"Me too."

"We need to go fill out some paperwork for the hospital," he said, "but I want to tell you kids something." He looked at Branson, Jewels, and me. "Don't waste any more time. Life is short, and none of us knows when someone's last day on earth will be. I hope you all know the Lord. If you do, please make witnessing to others your mission from now on."

Before we could respond, Kelly's mother said she wanted to see her son one more time, so they walked behind the curtain again.

I couldn't speak for Jewels or Branson, but I decided to accept the challenge. The next time someone I knew died, I wanted to be sure they had accepted Jesus Christ as their Savior.

"I'm going to the chapel," Branson said. He stood and strolled away. Jewels and I sat on the couch.

"It's hard to believe he's gone," she said.

"I know it hurts and you're going to miss him. But hopefully he's in a better place."

Jewels threw her arms around me, hugged me tightly, and sobbed. Then she whispered in a coarse voice, "Laurel, I prayed the salvation prayer."

"You did?" I squeaked, my heart racing. "When?"

"When you were performing CPR on Kelly. I guess I hoped it would help you save him."

"Jewels, that's awesome," I squealed.

"But my prayer didn't help Kelly."

Stroking her hair, I said, "There's nothing you or I could have done to prevent him from dying."

We sat in silence for a while. Then Jewels whispered, "My sin killed Kelly." She buried her head in my shoulder.

I held her in my arms and prayed the Lord would give me the right words to say. "God wasn't pleased with you having sex with Kelly," I told her, "but that didn't kill him."

She stood, tears streaking her makeup. "Then why did he die?"

"I don't know." I stood beside her and squeezed her hand. "Maybe Kelly accepted Christ years ago but wasn't living like he should."

Jewels sat back on the couch. "I want to see him again, in heaven."

"I hope you will." Sitting beside her, I placed my arms around her and gently patted her back. "It's OK to hope he knew the Lord. But now we've got to honor what his father said and tell everyone we know about Jesus."

"Definitely," she said, wiping her tears. "For Kelly."

"For God," I said.

"Yes," she replied. "For God."

When Jewels and I walked back into the fraternity house after leaving the hospital, we were bombarded with classmates pleading for us to confirm that Kelly was alive. It hurt to tell them otherwise and view the disappointment and horror on their faces.

Some grief counselors from Campus Outreach showed up to pray with us. After a lot of deep discussion, we all calmed down a little and decided to try to get some sleep. I witnessed to three people before I let Branson put his jacket under my head and convince me to rest.

After I lay down, he placed a blanket over Jewels's legs, then settled on the floor between us.

"Something's really changed you," I whispered to him. "I've never known you to be so . . . attentive."

"I'm just concerned, that's all," he said.

"I think there's more to it than that."

He shrugged. "I guess I'm looking at life a little differently these days. When Bo had his accident, and then accepted the Lord even though he can't ever walk again, that really hit me. The joy he found is something I've longed for all my life. Tonight, I realized that I can be here one minute and gone the next. That made me realize I need to get myself together."

"God's knocking on the door of your heart, Branson," I said, my heart racing. "If you're unsure about your salvation, let Him in. Make it real this time."

"I'm ready," he said, smiling at me. "I want to allow God into my heart."

"That's great."

"Can you help me do it?" he asked.

"How about I say a prayer and you can repeat after me," I suggested.

"OK."

I took his hand in mine. As I prayed, he repeated my words.

"Dear Lord, I know I'm a sinner. Without accepting Your Son, Jesus Christ, I can't go to heaven when I die. I believe that Jesus died on the cross for my sins, and that He rose again. Thank You for Your grace. In Jesus' name I pray, amen."

When I opened my eyes, I saw Branson staring at me. "Is that it?" he asked.

"Romans 10:13 says that everyone who calls on the name on the Lord will be saved."

Branson closed his eyes again and whispered a prayer of his own, in words from his heart. I listened excitedly. What an awesome blessing it was to help someone into the family of God!

Shortly after I returned to my dorm room that afternoon, Jewels's parents showed up to take her and her older sister, Julie Anne, out to dinner. Jewels had been shaking and crying off and on all day. I prayed her parents could comfort her.

I took a shower, and as I was toweling my hair, Payton came in. Her left eye was dark blue and maroon. My jaw dropped. "What happened?"

"You'd better sit down," Payton said as she touched her eye with her fingertips. "You're not going to believe this."

We sat on the edges of our beds and faced each other.

"Tad and I went to this club," she said, "and a bunch of

UGA football players were there. Suddenly Dakari and this guy on the SGA cabinet started fighting. Pretty soon a bunch of other guys got into the brawl. I got caught in the crossfire."

"Are you all right?"

She shrugged. "Tad took me to the infirmary to get my eye examined. While we were waiting for the doctor, the campus police came in. They accused Tad of hitting me."

"Why would they think he did it?" I asked.

"They said they've had a lot of cases of date violence this year."

"Oh, no," I breathed.

"I assured them that Tad hadn't harmed me, so they didn't arrest him. After the doctor released me, Tad started to take me home. But then Robyn called me on my cell phone. She told me she was still at the club, and someone there had been shot."

My heart sank

"I told Tad, and he turned the car around and raced back there."

I braced myself for the details.

"When we arrived, we saw police everywhere. Most of them were standing around a body covered with a sheet on the pavement between two cars. As soon as Tad and I got out of his car, Robyn ran over to us and told us that Dakari's brother, Drake, had been killed."

"Oh, my God," I cried.

Payton nodded. "After the police took Drake's body away in a coroner's van, I saw Dakari kneeling on the ground, crying uncontrollably. Tad told me to go home with Robyn. As we left the scene, I turned around and saw Tad embracing Dakari."

I hugged my roommate tight. Then I told her what had happened to Kelly at the fraternity party. We got down on our knees and prayed. We asked the Lord not to leave our sides and to give us the strength we needed to get through this time in our lives.

A couple of days later, Jewels came into my room carrying six black dresses. "I bought these yesterday," she said, her eyes red. "Which one do you think I should wear to Kelly's funeral?" She spread the dresses on my bed.

I chose the most conservative one.

"Part of him will be with me always," she said, "since he was my first."

I thanked God I'd never given Branson what Jewels had given Kelly.

Jewels gathered up the dresses. "After I take these other five back to the store, I'll pick you up for the service."

"You're taking the dresses back?"

She nodded. "I didn't know which one I'd want to wear, so I bought them all."

I gulped. Each of those dresses must have cost at least two hundred dollars. My credit card sure didn't have that high a limit.

After Jewels left, I looked in my closet and found a black suit. Before I could change into it, the phone rang.

"Sweetie," Mom said, "I've got some bad news."

I plopped down on the bed, not sure I could stand more bad news. Then I remembered God wouldn't put more on me than I could bear. "What is it?" I asked, my lower lip trembling.

"Granddad Shadrach started bleeding from his mouth this morning. Your grandmother rushed him to the hospital."

"Can I go see him?" I asked.

"We could pick you up in about two hours. If we drive all night, we can get there by morning."

"I'll be ready," I said, then hung up the phone in a daze.

I dropped to my knees, still holding the black suit. *Lord, please help my grandfather out of this.*

101

I heard a knock at my door. When I opened it I saw Jill and Mandelyn, two of my sorority sisters who lived upstairs.

"We heard about Kelly," Jill said as she hugged me.

"He was too young to die," Mandelyn said as she sat on my bed.

"Guys, I can't make it to the funeral," I said. "My grandfather isn't doing too well and I have to go home to see him." I hung my suit back in the closet. "You two have to be there for Jewels, OK?"

They agreed and sandwiched me between them with love.

———————

My whole family was piled in the van: Mom, Dad, Liam, Lance, Luke, and me. It reminded me of Christmas. But this time there was no fighting.

Liam took my hand. "I've been praying for your strength, Sis. I'm here if you need me."

Luke and Lance, who were sitting in the back row of seats behind me and Liam, leaned forward. Lance stroked my hair and Luke rubbed my shoulders. I appreciated my brothers' concern for me.

Lord, I prayed, *help me find a way to get through to my grandfather. I want him to know You.*

It would be much easier for me to deal with whatever came if Granddad was saved. Then it would be no problem accepting God's will.

possessing true joy

though it was a sad occasion, I was excited to be with my family again. As we drove to Arkansas in the middle of the night to see my father's father, my brothers and my mom slept. I helped Dad stay awake by chatting with him from the backseat.

"I love you," I said as I put my hand on his shoulder.

"I love you, too, sweetie," he said, tapping my fingers. "Everything's going to be fine."

"Yeah, I know," I told him as I placed a kiss on his cheek.

"How's school been going for you?" he asked.

"My grades are still good. I did pretty well on my midterms."

"Great. How are you doing emotionally? Your mom told me you tried to save some young man's life."

"But I wasn't able to," I said. "I keep wondering if I could have done more."

"At least you tried. If it wasn't his time, God would have allowed you to save him."

"I know you're right. But it's still hard."

My dad nodded. "Your mom said this happened in Columbia. What were you doing there?"

I hesitated, knowing he'd be disappointed. "I was at a fraternity party."

In a hard voice, he said, "Laurel, I'm not sending you to college so you can go partying. You're there to get an education. I understand you need to have some recreation, but there's always a lot of drinking at fraternity parties. That's hardly what I would consider a wholesome recreational activity." My dad turned to give me a stern glance and the car swerved a bit.

"Pay attention to the road, Dad," I said, hoping to change the topic of conversation.

After getting the car back on track, my father said, "I'm very proud of the young lady you've become. And I want you to continue in the right direction. I know you're walking with God, but the devil will always present obstacles, and you need to make the right choices. Some decisions you can't take back. So be smart."

"I understand, Dad," I replied.

"Good. I love you, Laurel," he said as he grasped my hand.

I grinned at my overprotective father. "Thanks for being so concerned."

At about three in the morning, we pulled into the parking lot at Memorial Hospital. My dad's two brothers and one sister, who all lived in Texas, were sitting in the waiting room watching TV and reading magazines, their faces lined with worry.

When we walked into Granddad's room in ICU, my grandmother sobbed with joy. My grandfather was connected to several machines and had an IV in his arm. A clear plastic mask covered his mouth and nose. I didn't know if he was asleep or unconscious.

"How's he doing?" my dad asked.

"He has a bleeding ulcer," my grandmother told us. "But the doctor said he's going to be OK." She buried her head into my father's chest and wept.

It was hard for me to believe that this man I thought was invincible could possibly die. Until that moment, I had never fully realized that he might not always be there for me. For the first time, I seriously wondered how I would go on without my grandpa.

We all trudged to the waiting room and eventually fell asleep in the chairs. When the sun peered through the windows, I woke up and realized all of my relatives were still there except my parents. I rushed to Granddad's room and found them sitting next to his bed, speaking to him and holding his hands.

"He's still with us," my father told me as I entered the cold, sterile room. "He's been asking to see all of you."

I turned around and saw my brothers standing behind me.

"He can't have too many visitors at one time," Dad said.

Liam and Luke agreed to wait. They followed Mom and Dad into the hall, leaving Lance and me to visit with Granddad.

I looked into his pale face. I touched his hand; it was cold. When he opened his eyes, I leaned over and stroked his unkempt hair and told him I loved him.

He pulled off his oxygen mask. "My sweet Laurel," he said in a scratchy voice. "And Lance, my boy." He started coughing, and it took a few minutes for him to compose himself. Lance asked him if we should get the nurse.

He shook his head and smiled. "I've got some good news for you." I held my breath. "Your dad and I had a long talk earlier today. We both realize my days on this earth are numbered. This might sound crazy, but I heard Jesus calling me to Him. It was like He was pounding on my heart, wanting to come into my life. So I let Him in."

I started to cry, happy that Grandpa had finally accepted Christ but sad that he didn't have much longer to live on earth.

"I know He's in me now," my grandfather said. "He has forgiven me for every one of my sins." He glanced at Lance, then looked my way. "I know you kids will be fine without me."

"Don't talk like that, Granddad," Lance said.

"Everything is in order," he said in a weak voice.

"But you're going to be OK," I said, squeezing his frail white hand as hard as I could without disturbing the IV. "The doctor said so."

"Come closer," he said. I did, and he gave me a big hug. "Life is precious," he whispered in my ear. "If you want things in life, you have to go after them. Don't wait for them to come to you."

I told Granddad I would take his advice and that he needed to get some rest. Lance squeezed Granddad's hand. Then the two of us walked out of the room, and Liam and Luke took our places.

I started crying as we walked down the hall to the waiting room. Lance put his arm around me and told me everything was going to be all right.

I stopped by the bathroom and washed my face with cold water so my parents and relatives wouldn't see that I'd been crying. Nothing was wrong with showing pain, but I wanted to be strong for them.

When I left the bathroom, Lance was waiting for me. We walked back to the visitors area together, where we joined the rest of the family.

After sitting in the waiting room for about an hour, my brothers and I decided to go back to my grandparents' house to rest. No one said anything on the drive to the house. When we got there, my brothers decided to watch television, but I took a nap.

When I woke up about five hours later, Dad told me that Granddad had left this world in his sleep. It hurt worse than anything I could remember, but knowing that he had given his life to Christ made it a little easier. I was thankful that my grandfather was in a place of complete peace. One day we would be together. He was with Jesus, and that was exciting.

We all held up remarkably well at the funeral. We knew where Granddad's soul was going, and that was cause for rejoicing. As my grandmother viewed her husband's body, she squeezed my hand. "I'm going to see him again, honey. I never knew letting him go was going to be this easy. But I'm ready to go too."

Of course she'd had more time on this earth than I had, but I knew my time could come before hers. I was glad my grandmother was ready for heaven, though I sure didn't want to let her go.

As my grandfather's body was taken out of the church, I looked at my grandmother's face. There I saw peace and even joy.

Over the years I had seen my father commit many bodies to the ground. He always told the grieving families that they should rejoice if their loved ones were believers. People often told him he would feel different when he had to bury someone he loved. But he was just as happy for his dad as he'd been for all the others he had ushered into heaven.

When it was my turn, I took the white rose that the funeral director gave to me and placed it on Granddad's casket.

Lord, I prayed, *thank You for letting me know such a great man, and thank You for letting him know You.*

I looked at the casket. *Thanks for loving me all these years,* I told my grandfather. *I'll see you soon.*

When we got back to Georgia and I had to go back to school, I had a hard time saying good-bye to my family. But I was excited about getting back to my world.

As I started to unpack my things, Payton came in.

"You're back," she said, giving me a hug. "I'm so sorry about your grandfather."

I rested my head on her shoulder. Though I hadn't shed a tear up to that moment, when I heard Payton sobbing, I couldn't hold back.

"I know you miss your granddad," Payton said, "'cause I miss mine. Let it out, girl. You don't have to be strong for me."

After hearing those words of support and comfort from Payton, I let all the tears I had been holding inside fall. Payton held me and told me everything was going to be OK.

After my tears subsided, Payton and I went to the gym. If we were going to make a real run at the cheerleading thing, we had to get serious. We were still having problems with different parts of the routine we were preparing, and the tryouts were coming up real fast. Payton showed me what she called a simple dance step. But it had so many parts of the body moving at the same time, I couldn't copy it.

"I can't do that," I yelled, pacing the floor.

"Yes, you can," she said. "Let me show you again." She repeated the moves extra slowly.

I tried again, but ended up falling on my bottom. Maybe pom-poms and megaphones weren't for me after all.

"I give up," I shouted in despair. "I'll never get this."

Payton grabbed my hand, pulled me to my feet, and we tried again. And again. And again. When I finally got it, both of us started jumping up and down and screaming at the top of our lungs.

It was Payton's turn to learn from me, so I showed her how to do a double back handspring. When she tried, she landed on her back. She lay there groaning in pain, but I could tell she was OK.

"Come on, Payton, you can do it. You just need to keep practicing. Let's do this until it's perfect."

She laughed. Then she tried again. Pretty soon her jumps got higher, her execution improved, and her confidence grew stronger.

To celebrate, we headed to Baskin-Robbins. "So," I asked Payton after we chose our flavors and took a table in the back corner, "what's been going on with you while I was away?"

"Drake's funeral was tough."

"How's Dakari?"

"Not good. I tried telling him about God, but since his brother wasn't saved, he didn't really want to hear it."

"Have you seen Jewels much?" I asked.

"She's been talking to me a little, and to Robyn a lot. I'm worried about her, though. She hasn't seemed quite right since Kelly died."

"I'll try to talk to her today," I said, licking my butter pecan sugar cone.

"You really care about Jewels, don't you?" Payton asked, wiping her mouth with a napkin.

"Yeah," I admitted. "She gives me a hard time, and she makes it pretty difficult to love her, but I do see her changing." Payton nodded. "Hey, you want to go see a matinee?"

"Sure. Let's make a day of it. After the movie we can go to the mall and hang out and act crazy like we did when we were in high school."

As we walked back to her car, I asked, "How are you and Tad doing?"

"We're doing OK," she said. We got into the car and left the parking lot. "You really should go on a blind date with Tad and me."

"We'll see," I said, even though I was thinking, No way.

She started babbling on about this friend of Tad's she wanted me to go out with. Though he did sound intriguing, my heart belonged to another.

We went to the movies, the mall, and out to dinner. When we got back to the room, she immediately got on the phone with Tad. As Payton discussed the double date with him, I was kicking myself for not telling her about Charlie. I needed to let her know how I felt about him.

She was still on the phone with Tad when the time came for me to leave for my study date with Charlie at the library. I waved to her as I left the room, deciding I'd have to tell her about him later.

As I got close to the library, I started having a funny feeling. It had been over a week since I'd seen Charlie, and my life had changed so much. My grandfather had died, Payton and I were on the right track with our cheerleading tryout routine, and my roommate and I were hanging out together again. What if Charlie's life had changed as well? What if he'd needed me and I wasn't around?

Smiling at the library workers, I proceeded toward the elevator. But the door closed before I could get there, so I had to wait for the next one.

When I got upstairs I dashed to our usual table. It was empty. I stared at it as if Charlie might appear before my eyes if I looked long enough. But the view didn't change. So I slammed my books down.

The usual gang was sitting at the next table. "Want to join us?" Danny asked in a playful tone.

I sat down in my regular seat, opened a textbook, and stared at the pages, totally ignoring Danny because I didn't want to be the brunt of a joke.

"We've missed you," Danny teased.

I continued ignoring him.

"Where have you been?" he asked.

I turned the page of the textbook.

"Are you all right?" Danny asked. "We've been worried. Your friend's been going crazy wondering where you were."

"Really?" I said, looking up. "Has he been looking for me?"

110

"He's been coming here every day, bugging us about you. Why haven't you been around?"

Tears started to form in my eyes. "My grandfather passed away."

"I'm sorry," Danny said in a caring voice.

"I'm sorry too," a voice behind me said.

I turned around and looked into Charlie's eyes. When I jumped up from the table, he hugged me tight. Then he kissed me softly on the cheek. I melted.

"Do you really need to study?" he asked. "Or can we go somewhere?"

"Let's go."

He grabbed my books and we exited the library, waving at the library workers, who smiled at us.

"Do you want to get a soda?" he asked.

"I'm open. I'm just happy to see you."

Charlie stopped walking. "We can sit right here on this bench and look at the stars."

We sat on the bench and he held my hand.

"Is everything OK?" he asked.

"Yeah," I assured him. "I'm sorry for not calling you. But my grandfather passed away. It all happened very quickly."

"I'm sorry."

"It's all right. Really. My Granddad Shadrach didn't believe in God most of his life, but just before he died, he accepted Christ into his heart."

Charlie gave me a huge smile. "That's great."

"Yeah, it is."

"I missed you," he said, giving me a warm hug. "But now that you're back, I'm possessing true joy."

resting
and relaxing

two days later Payton and I were back in the gym trying to make ourselves competitive enough for the cheerleading finals. I was too exhausted to keep up with her dance moves. So I sat on the gym floor with a towel draped over my head, sipping cold water from my jug.

"C'mon, girl," Payton said as she jogged up to me. "You gotta keep up."

"No way," I said, not moving. "Not unless you try another flip."

She plopped down beside me. "Where's my water?"

I laughed. "I'm a bad influence on you."

"Do you think we should quit?"

"Not yet." I sipped some more water.

Finally, we got up to try again. We encouraged each other to do our best. I managed to get six of eight beats down, and Payton landed her first back handspring. We were so excited, we high-fived each other and then hugged. Then we celebrated our success by taking another break.

After several gulps of water, Payton said, "I've got to tell you what I'm gonna do to Tad for April Fool's Day tomorrow."

"This ought to be good," I said with a grin.

"I'm gonna tell him I don't want to be his girlfriend anymore. I haven't talked to him in a few days, so he'll probably believe it. He'll be all messed up."

I frowned. "My brother Lance is a big April Fool's person. But a lot of times his tricks get him into trouble. I don't want to see that happen to you."

"Well, Tad is due for payback because he got me good last year," she said with a smirk.

It was obvious I wasn't going to convince her to forget about this, so I kept my mouth shut.

Shortly after midnight Payton played her little trick on her boyfriend. He hung up on her. She waited an hour for him to call her back, but he didn't. She called him to say, "April Fool's!" but before she could get the words out, he told her they didn't have anything to discuss and that she should stop calling him.

Panicked, she asked me over and over if I thought everything was going to be OK. She paced our small room relentlessly, even biting her nails, which I'd never seen her do.

Somehow I drifted off to sleep. When I woke up, I saw Payton asleep.

"Hey," I hollered at her, "you're gonna miss your class."

Her eyes popped open. "I've got a test today," she shrieked as she jumped out of bed. Then she looked at the clock.

When I said, "April Fool's," she glared at me. "Hey, you're the one who loves jokes," I added.

She groaned and lay back down.

"I thought it was funny," I mumbled.

Later that morning, as I walked to class with Jewels, she told me there was something she needed to talk to me about.

"Lately," she said, "Branson has really been there for me. Not that we're boyfriend and girlfriend or anything, but there's something special he brings to my life. With everything that happened between you two last semester, I thought I should ask you if it was OK if we become . . . you know, friends."

I busted up laughing. "Pretty good April Fool's joke," I said. "But you can't get me."

She blinked. "I'm serious."

I stared at her. She really did look serious. But I wasn't sure how to answer her. It did kinda bother me to think of them being friends. I hated myself for wanting to hold on to something I had already let go of. But the thought of Jewels being with Branson made me uncomfortable.

"Oh, gosh, look at the time," I said, glancing at the clock on the wall. "I've got to get to class." I dashed off before she could say anything more.

On the way to my class I prayed, *Lord, help me. Something's not right here. I know that whatever You're doing with Branson and Jewels should be fine by me, but it's not. I guess I'm not completely resting in You, and I don't like that.*

"What are you planning to do for spring break?" I asked Payton after we finished our practice in the gym.

"I don't know," she said, wiping her forehead with a towel. "Some of my friends from high school want to go visit a friend of ours in upstate New York."

"That sounds like fun."

"How about you?"

"I need to stay here and work on my dance moves."

Payton sighed. "I'm burned out from all this practice. If I can't tumble now, a couple more weeks won't matter."

"I guess not," I said with a shrug.

"You sound down. What's going on?"

I told her about the jealousy that had been raging inside me ever since Jewels told me about liking Branson. "I thought I was over him, but I still feel weird about him liking someone else."

"I'm going through something similar," she said. "I've been pretty agitated with Robyn ever since she got paired up with Dakari during recruiting weekends."

"So what do we do?" I asked, sitting on the floor with my legs crossed.

"Maybe we should pray and give our ex-boyfriends to God. As Christians, we should want what's best for them."

"You're right."

"Robyn's a great girl. Dakari could do a lot worse than her. Maybe the same is true for Jewels and Branson."

"Maybe."

"Besides, who knows if either of those relationships will go down that road."

"I guess there's nothing to worry about then."

Before we got back to practicing, we asked the Lord to give us strength in our current relationships. It felt good to have someone who understood.

That evening Charlie and I went out on our second official date. He'd told me to wear a jogging suit, but didn't divulge where we were going.

When he arrived to pick me up, the first thing he did was wrap a silk scarf around my eyes. "Why are you blindfolding me?" I asked as he guided me along.

"It's a secret but it's one I know you'll like."

After a short walk, he led me into an elevator. From the motion, I could tell we were going up.

When he finally took off the scarf, I found myself in a football stadium suite with two TVs, a bar, a bathroom, twelve seats, and a cozy couch. We sat down on the couch, and soon a waiter came and served us steak, baked potatoes, and a salad.

"This is delicious," I said after I took my first bite.

"Glad you like it," he said, smiling.

"How did you pull this off?" I asked as I surveyed the room.

He grinned and kept chewing his steak.

"I'm guessing your dad's an important alumni or school administrator. Am I close?"

"Don't try to guess why or how, Lucy," he said quietly. "Just enjoy it."

I set my fork down on the linen cloth. "I'm tired of all the secrets," I said. "I want to know everything about you."

He stood, looked out the press-box window, then turned to me. "I want you to get comfortable seeing yourself in this stadium."

"Why?" I asked, frustrated at how little I really knew about this guy.

"Because when you make the cheerleading squad, you're going to be out there."

"*If* I make the squad," I muttered.

"I've got a special gift for you," he said. "Come here." He stood and extended his hand.

I placed my hand in his and he pulled me to my feet. He escorted me out of the suite and down the hall. We took an elevator to the field and stood together in the big open space. Charlie walked me to the fifty-yard line. "I want to see you do your flips."

"Right here?"

He nodded.

"OK," I said hesitantly. As I started performing my moves on the lush green grass, I realized how much I wanted to be a Georgia Bulldogs cheerleader. I tumbled between the fifty-yard line and the sidelines.

When I finished, Charlie gave me a standing ovation. Then he reached into his pocket and brought out a box wrapped in shiny white paper.

I opened the box. Inside was a clock made of cherry wood. On the face, just below the hands, was a cheerleader in a University of Georgia uniform. When I turned the clock over, I saw an inscription. It read, "Laurel Shadrach, UGA Cheerleader, 2003–2004." It was signed, "Love, your Charlie."

"Over the top?" he asked.

"No, it's cute." I gave him a kiss on the cheek. "Thank you."

Knowing he believed in me made me believe it too.

Boy, it felt good to lay my head back on the edge of the tub and feel the warm, peppermint-scented bathwater soothe my body. Payton, Jewels, and Robyn had left for spring break and I was really enjoying having the space all to myself. I closed my eyes and pretended I was in a Jacuzzi. My aching muscles released the tension from all the practice I'd been putting in. As the water started getting cool, I let some of it out and ran more.

Suddenly I thought about my old suite mate Anna. She'd tried to end her life in the same tub I was in. She was a sweet girl who didn't see anything good in herself. I needed to call her.

As I started to get out of the tub, my phone rang.

"Hey, girl," I heard a familiar voice say.

"Brittany?"

"And me," another voice said.

"Meagan?"

Wrapping a towel around my wet body, I asked, "What are you guys up to?"

"I'm on spring break, and Meagan's still carrying that baby," Brittany said.

"Where are you?" I asked, water dripping from my hair to the floor.

"We're in Athens," Meagan said. "Give us directions so we can pick you up."

I told them how to get to my dorm, then scurried around the room getting dressed and ready.

The first thing out of Brittany's mouth when she walked in the door was, "I can't believe you live in the dorm."

"Why not?" I said. "Don't you?"

She gave me a patronizing smile. "I have an apartment."

When Meagan stepped out from behind Brittany, I noticed that her stomach was getting big. I reached out to touch it, but Meagan stepped back.

"Don't make a big deal out of it," she said.

"Where's a good place to eat around here?" Brittany asked.

I took my friends to a tavern restaurant that claimed to serve the best hot wings in Georgia. Brittany smiled at the surroundings, the food choices, and the cute waiters. Meagan stared at the menu and said she wasn't very hungry.

"C'mon, Meagan, you've got to try the wings here," I said.

"No, thanks. Spicy food doesn't agree with the baby. I think I'll just have a BLT."

After we placed our orders, Brittany announced, "Meagan found a family for her baby."

"You did?" I squealed.

"Yeah," Meagan said as she adjusted her shirt. "This guy who used to play football for UGA has three adopted children and his wife wants one more."

"How did you find him?"

"I was baby-sitting at a conference for Professional Athletes Outreach. This guy and his wife started talking with me when they came to pick up their kids, and I found out they were signed up with the same adoption agency I've been working with. They don't live too far from the Georgia–Florida line. So after I have the baby I can go back to school and maybe even baby-sit for them sometimes. That way I'll be able to see my child."

"That sounds great," I said.

"I think so," she said as she stared at a couple and their baby a few tables away. "The way this whole thing worked out tells me there's a purpose for my pregnancy. I mean, I know it was wrong to have sex before I got married. But God didn't abandon me just because I sinned. He still loves me, and I know He has a plan for my baby."

"I'm trying to convince her to come back to school after the kid's born," Brittany told me. "I really miss this girl."

"Yeah, right," Meagan said. "You're going to be too busy if you make the cheerleading squad."

My eyes popped wide. "You're trying out for cheerleading?"

"Yeah," she said with a grin.

"Me too!"

"No way," Brittany said. "With all those flips you do, you'll be great."

"Thanks," I said. "But there are some dance moves I can't seem to get down. I've been practicing a lot, but I have no rhythm."

"I can show you some moves if you'll show me some flips."

After lunch, we all went to the school gym and started working out together. Meagan, who'd been a cheerleader herself in high school, coached us.

After a great workout, Brittany offered to treat us to a manicure and pedicure. It was such a treat to hang out with my friends and enjoy an entire day without stress, just resting and relaxing.

helping them out

"don't keep us in suspense," Brittany said to me as the nail stylist painted her toes. "We came up here to find out what's going on with you."

"What do you mean?" I asked, relaxing my feet in the bubbling hot water.

Brittany placed her feet by the fan. "Branson's been home for a few days, and he said you guys are really, really over."

Meagan placed her fingernails under the light to let them dry. "We figure you've got someone else. And we want to know all about him."

Brittany inspected her toenails. "I don't like this color," she whined. "Take it off and just do clear."

The stylist obliged her. Brittany was a difficult customer, but I knew she tipped well. Meagan was the opposite. I missed them both.

Hanging out with my friends felt like old times, but I

knew they'd tell Branson everything I said. Had he told them he'd been hanging out with my suite mate? I didn't want to mention that. No need to stir up confusion.

"Yes, there is a guy," I admitted.

"I knew it," Brittany chirped.

"Details, please," Meagan said.

"We met at the library. We've been out on a couple of dates. He's really nice and smart, and he cares about me. And he's majorly cute."

"Muscular?" Meagan asked.

"Yeah." I smiled. "But most important, he cares about God."

"Not in a geeky way, I hope," Meagan said, "like your brother Liam."

"Why would you say that?" I asked, remembering the close relationship they had once shared. My oldest brother really liked my good friend till she decided he was "too Christian." Then she fell for the bad-boy image she saw in my other brother, Lance. I had really been mad at her for toying with my brothers' affections. But thankfully, we'd managed to get through it and remain friends.

"Liam called me the other day," Meagan said. "He asked how was I was doing. But before I could answer, he started forcing God down my throat. He sounded just like my mom. It was annoying. Foster was kind of like that, too, right? That's why you broke up with him, isn't it?"

"Sort of," I said, trying to find the right words. "It was more that Foster had a stronger walk with God than I did. He needed someone who was on the same spiritual level with him."

"Well," Meagan said, "Liam told me he had something important to talk to you about, but when he got all preachy on me, I hung up before he could tell me what it was. So you might want to call him."

"Can I borrow your cell?" I asked.

"Sure," Meagan said, handing me her phone.

I called home. Even before I could ask Liam what was up, he told me he needed a soloist who could sing soprano for the Sunday service that week. Then he said, "Dad's been kind of down ever since we got back from Arkansas, and I figured hearing you sing would put a smile on his face."

I didn't have to think about it for long. "I'll just come home with my girlfriends today," I said, "after we finish getting our nails done."

Meagan and Brittany were thrilled about spending more time with me. I didn't want our time together to end either.

They teased me all the way back to Conyers about my new beau. They thought it was hilarious that I didn't know his real name. Brittany jokingly offered to look him up on the Internet. I was dying for more details about my mysterious Prince Charming, but I wanted them to come from him. Knowing Brittany, she would only dig for dirt. I didn't want her doing anything to mess things up.

I arrived home to the smell of turkey and all the sides. Mom had prepared the big spread as soon as Liam told her I was coming home.

"We miss you," she said. "We were so disappointed when you didn't come home for spring break. I'm glad your brother convinced you to change your mind. This is going to make your father so happy." She held me tight, letting me know I was making her happy too.

That night I practiced the song with Liam that we were going to perform on Sunday. I was really excited when Luke told me that Liam had written it.

"It's beautiful," I told him.

Liam patted me on the back. "I'm glad you agreed to sing it because no one else was doing it justice."

"Placing Others Before Me" was the title of the song. It fit my situation. By coming home to sing my brother's song, I was doing just that. He needed me so I was there.

When my dad came into the house, he slammed his briefcase onto the kitchen table and stalked into his study, slamming the door behind him. I wanted to try to help my father. After all the times he'd helped me, I figured it was my turn. But I needed God's assistance. I knew He could help me bring a smile to my dad's face.

I retreated to my old room, knelt beside my bed, and started praying. *Lord, give me the words to say to my dad. Something is going on with him. I know he misses his father. He taught us to be excited about going to be with You. But maybe it's different when you lose one of your parents. Thanks in advance for all Your help and all Your love. In Jesus' name. Amen.*

"I want to practice the song one more time," Liam said, startling me from the doorway.

"In a minute," I said, grabbing my brush off the dresser and running it through my hair. "Hey, why haven't one of you guys moved into my room? I mean, the three of you shouldn't still be cramped up in that one little room."

My brother looked around. "I guess it just still seems like yours, all girly and everything. I'm just gonna be here a few more months anyway. Besides, with everything that's been going on, the three of us have actually been tight."

"Even you and Lance?"

Liam nodded.

I turned from the mirror. "Where is he anyway?"

"Football practice."

"Is he still the starting quarterback?"

"Yeah," Liam said with little enthusiasm. "So, are you ready to practice?"

I thought about seeing my dad first, but then I thought that maybe if he heard me practice, that could be the ice breaker that got the two of us talking. Daddy loved hearing me sing. Liam and I went back to the piano.

After I sang the first verse, Dad appeared in the doorway, smiling. I stopped the song and rushed into his arms. He hugged me tight.

"Let's go sit on the porch," I suggested, starting toward the front door.

Dad and I had always loved sitting on the porch together. When we first moved to Georgia, I hated Conyers, so I spent a lot of time on the porch swinging and pouting. My dad would come and sit by me and ask me to sing a praise song. Once I started, the bitterness would melt away.

"So," I said, sitting beside him, "what's weighing you down?"

He just stared at me and sighed.

I tilted my head. "I want to help you, but I can't if you don't tell me what's on your mind."

"Gosh, you sound like me," he said, smiling.

"That's because I had a good teacher." I punched him in the arm.

He rubbed his arm as if I'd hurt him. After a few quiet swings, he spoke quietly. "I really regret not spending more time with my dad when he was here."

I rubbed his back. It hurt me to see him fall apart like this when I couldn't do anything to ease his pain.

"I really miss my little girl too," he added. "I've never been as close to the boys as I have been to you." My father told me how strained his relationship was with my brothers, especially Lance.

My stomach felt unsettled.

Tears formed in my father's eyes. "I don't want to wake up one day and find out it's too late. I help people every day, but I can't seem to get through to my own family."

I gazed into my dad's face. "Granddad had a weird way of showing he loved us, but we all know he did. The boys know you love them too. So ease up on yourself a little. I mean, we can always do more, but the things you do for your family are appreciated, even if we don't always tell you so."

My dad smiled. "Thanks. It feels good to hear you say that. And you're right about my dad's love for us. His will proved that." He patted my knee. "Baby, you don't have to try out for the cheerleading squad. Granddad left us enough money to pay for four years of tuition for you and your brothers."

"Wow," I said. I hadn't realized Granddad had that kind of money. "You know, I really appreciate the offer. But I'm trying out for cheerleading because I want to, not just for the scholarship. I may have to use that money if I don't make the team. But Payton and I have really been practicing, and if I say so myself, I think we're starting to look pretty good."

Dad assured me that even if I didn't make the squad, I would still be able to be a Georgia Bulldog student. I thanked him, then sang the first verse of one of my dad's favorite songs, "Lead Me, Lord, Lead Me." It was my way of saying that we were both weak and needed God to lead us out of the darkness we were in. When I finished singing, my dad gave me a huge hug.

"Everything's going to work out," I told him, hugging him back. "All we have to do is give everything we go through in life to God."

"You're right, honey. I can even trust Him to show me how to get through to my boys."

"That's right," I said. "So you can quit beating yourself up about that."

Lance pulled the car into the driveway, then jumped out and bounded up the steps. He grabbed me, picked me up off the porch swing, kissed me on the cheek, then told me he missed having me around. I assured him I missed him too.

After dinner Lance and I went out to the backyard and lay in the double-wide hammock.

"So, what's going on with you?" I asked.

"Just the usual," he said. "A lot of pressure leading the football team, keeping my grades up, and paying off all those gambling debts."

"You know Dad wants to help, don't you?"

"Dad?" Lance scoffed. "He's too busy with the church and worrying about Luke and Liam. He's not focused on me." Lance gazed up at the stars.

"That's not true," a hoarse voice said. We both looked up and saw Dad standing in the doorway. "I care deeply for you, Lance. If there's any way I can be there for you, I want to."

Lance jumped out of the hammock to hug Dad. As he did, the hammock flipped over and dumped me onto the hard ground. When my backside hit, my brother and my dad just about fell over laughing. I ran into the house, rubbing my bottom, but smiling too. I was excited that the two of them were bonding.

I found Mom in the kitchen washing dishes. "Take a break," I told her, grabbing a towel out of the drawer. "I'll do that."

"Actually, I'd love your help," she said, handing me a wet saucepan. As I started drying it, she asked, "How's cheerleading going?"

"I'm working hard at it."

"And the sorority?" Mom asked.

"We've got some public service stuff coming up. I'm excited about helping others."

"If there's anything I can do for you, just let me know."

We did the dishes in silence for a few moments, and I started to sense that my mom wasn't as perky as she usually was. Hoping she would feel comfortable sharing what was on her heart with me, I asked, "Are you and Dad OK?"

She gave me a beautiful smile. "Yes," she said. "But I am glad you came home when you did. Your father and I talked while you were out back with Lance. You may not realize it, but you touched a part of him tonight that I've been trying to get at for weeks." She placed her soapy hands on my face. "I'm so thankful for you."

"And I'm thankful to have a wonderful family."

Mom hugged me. "Let's make a pot of tea."

126

I nodded, eager to share a warm drink with my mother. While she filled the kettle with water and put it on the stove, I grabbed the canister of teabags and pulled two spoons out of the drawer.

"How are your friends at school?" Mom asked as she stood by the stove.

"Jewels is doing good," I said, opening a green-mint teabag. "It was hard for her when her boyfriend Kelly died, but that showed her that she needs something more in her life. Robyn is starting to like Payton's ex-boyfriend Dakari. And I think Jewels likes Branson."

"Really?" Mom brought the whistling kettle to the table. "How do you feel about that?" It was good to have girl talk with my mom. We were friends and our bond was priceless.

"You know, it doesn't really bother me as much as it used to," I said as she poured steaming water into our cups.

I told Mom how remarkable Charlie was.

"He sounds like a wonderful young man," Mom said as she sat down and placed her hand over mine. "Oh, Laurel, I've missed you. Thanks for spending the day with us. All these men are driving me crazy." We laughed.

"I miss you too. I'll try to come home more often. College is great, but home is the best."

"I can't believe all these girls don't have parents," I whispered to Jewels after giving an inspirational message to the Good Hope Group Home for Girls. My sorority had volunteered to mentor the twelve- to eighteen-year-old orphans.

"I know," Jewels said. "This is really depressing."

The worn-down group home, with its peeling paint, broken front step, and ripped screen door, housed forty-two girls, most of them African-American. Some sat around smoking cigarettes and playing cards, while others were dancing to videos on television.

We met one girl who looked like she was in her early

127

twenties. We were told she was only fifteen and she'd been abused and abandoned by her mother, who was a crack addict.

When we first arrived, the young girls had been apprehensive about getting close to us. But when we started talking about some of the latest videos, and singing and dancing to the music, they finally started responding.

We got to know them better by helping those who needed it. Mandelyn tutored a few of the girls. Jewels painted the girls' nails. Jill handed out clothes we'd collected at our sorority house. I talked with a small group about how peer pressure can affect a young woman's progress in life. Our collaborative effort made me feel proud to be a Alpha Gamma Delta.

A tall, slim girl named Ashanti came up to me when I was finished talking. "Y'all alright."

"Thanks," I responded, pretty sure that was a compliment.

"I'm feelin' all that positive stuff you said."

"Well, anything special you see in me is really the Holy Spirit inside me. Ashanti, do you believe in Jesus Christ?"

"Yeah," she said. "I was baptized two years ago."

"That's great," I said, hugging her. "If you let His light shine through you, you can be just as together as me." We laughed.

"You think I could holla at you sometime?" she asked shyly.

"I'd like that." I gave her my telephone number, and she promised to call me.

All too soon it was time to leave. After telling the girls good-bye, we walked outside the group home. Jill asked me what I was planning to do next.

"I've got to study," I told her.

"Me too," Mandelyn said.

"Let's all go to the library," Jewels suggested with a twinkle in her eye.

I didn't want them to go. Charlie didn't like sorority girls, and I didn't want him to see me with them.

"You guys don't have to go with me," I said. "I can get more studying done alone."

Before I knew it, Jewels, Jill, Mandelyn, and I were in the library sitting at a table on the second floor. It was an hour earlier than I usually came in, and I figured even if Charlie came in early, he'd take the elevator straight from the first to the third floor, so hopefully he wouldn't see me. To my surprise, the girls actually started studying.

I kept looking at the clock, trying to come up with an excuse to go to the third floor. When it was almost 7:30, and my friends seemed engrossed in their studying, I got up quietly and snuck across the room. But as I neared the elevator, I saw Tad at a table in the far corner with a girl. She was brown skinned, had long light brown hair, and wore a really tight, skimpy outfit. They had their textbooks open, but they weren't looking at the books. They were talking and laughing with each other.

I hoped Jewels wouldn't see them, because I knew she would tell Payton and imply that Tad was cheating on her. Fortunately, Jewels was busy reading her American Literature book. When I saw the girl tenderly touch Tad's cheek, I headed over there.

"Remember me?" I said to Tad.

He looked up. "You're Payton's roommate, right?"

"Oh, so you remember Payton, your girlfriend." I exaggerated the last word, glaring at the girl on his arm.

She gave me a smug look, then smiled at Tad. "I'll be right back. I have to go to the ladies' room." She glided her hands over his chest before standing.

"Is there something you want to say to me?" Tad asked me after she left.

I leaned in and whispered, "I'm sure you think this is none of my business, but my roommate loves you. I know you care for her, so what are you doing with someone else?"

"We were just studying," he claimed. "When was the last time you talked to Payton?"

I thought about that for a minute. "I haven't talked with her since break."

"I know," he said as he rearranged his books. "She was in Atlanta making trouble."

"I don't think she was making near as much trouble as you are," I told him, nodding at the ladies' room.

He stood and looked me in the eye. "Laurel, I'm here to study. Whatever you think you saw wasn't what it looked like. I am angry at Payton right now, but I'm not crazy."

"What could you possibly have to be angry about?" I fumed at him.

"That's between me and Payton," he shot back, "and I'd rather not go into it if you don't mind." He sat down and started reading his textbook. I turned around and stormed off to the bathroom.

When I entered I saw the girl from Tad's table washing her hands. "Hi," I said in a polite voice.

She glared at me. "Whatever," she grumbled, then turned back to the sink.

I leaned against the bathroom counter. "The guy you're with is my roommate's boyfriend. Your flirtation isn't going to work on him."

"First of all," she said, putting her wet hand in my face, "you need to stay out of my business. There ain't no ring on his finger, and he wasn't worried about his girlfriend when he was all up in my grill. If you think I'm gonna stop tryin' to get with Tad Taylor 'cause your girl is his girlfriend, you's crazy. You need to get outta my face while you still can."

She pushed me out of the way and headed for the door. Before she could leave, I stepped in front of her. "You'll just get hurt in the long run."

"Then that's my business," she growled.

"Fine," I said, stepping aside. "Don't let me hold up your studying."

As she threw open the door and strutted out, Payton walked in.

"You need to talk to your guy," I told her.

Payton started crying. "Laurel, I messed up. He's so mad at me. He thinks I let him down."

"Did you?"

"No!"

"Then tell him that. Now!" I practically shoved her out the door.

She wiped her tears and approached the table where Tad and the girl were sitting. I followed at a discreet distance.

I wondered what would happen next. Maybe pushing Payton into a tense situation wasn't the best idea I'd ever had. But I needed to do whatever I could to try to help them out.

releasing
the pressure

i followed Payton as she stomped over to Tad's table in
the library. That other girl was sitting with him, entirely
too close and cozy. I hoped my roommate wouldn't make a
scene.

When she reached Tad, Payton demanded that they go
outside to talk.

"I don't feel like it right now," he said. Then he stormed
off. The girl laughed in Payton's face and followed Tad out
of the library.

I touched Payton's shoulder. When she turned around I
saw anger in her eyes.

"I'm sorry," I said.

"I'm going home." She marched to the elevator and
punched the down button several times.

Lord, help her, I prayed.

I decided to rejoin my sorority sisters, although I kinda

wished they were gone so I could jet upstairs to see if Charlie was there.

I was glad I hadn't bumped into him when I was with my preppy friends. But I knew I was going to have to tell him about my affiliation eventually. *If he doesn't like sorority girls, then maybe I'm not the one for him.*

When I turned the corner, I saw my girlfriends still at the table. Jill elbowed Jewels's shoulder and pointed my way.

"Laurel, where have you been?" Jewels scolded. "You're supposed to be helping us study."

I sat down and tried to concentrate. But I kept checking my watch, wondering if Charlie was upstairs looking for me.

"You got an appointment or something?" Jill asked.

"Yeah," I said. "I mean, I love being with you guys, but I really have to go to the gym. Cheerleading tryouts are coming up soon." I gathered my stuff and started to leave. Everyone else in the group stood too.

"You guys can keep studying without me." Their books were still scattered on the table, so I knew it would be a while before they'd be ready to go. So before they had time to argue, I darted away. I took the stairs so they wouldn't know that I went up instead of down.

When I opened the door to the third floor, I saw Tad and that girl practically locked in a kiss. Before I could storm over there and give that cheating boy a piece of my mind, I saw him take the girl's hands off his shoulders and walk away.

"You ain't nothin' but a waste of time," she hollered after him. "If you don't want to get with me, then you and your little girlfriend can keep each other."

Tad marched to the elevator without looking back at her or even off to the side, where I was standing. When the door closed and the elevator started its descent, I raced down the steps to the first floor. I caught up to him at the library entrance and hollered for him to wait up. He stopped, but didn't turn around.

"I want you to know," I panted, out of breath from running down all those steps, "I told Payton she had nothing to worry about. I know you really care about her."

"Thanks," he said, stuffing his hands into his pants pockets. "But you were right. I should never have been with that girl."

I tried to comfort him by placing my hand on his shoulder, but he pulled away.

"Do you know where Payton is?" he asked.

"She said she was going back to the dorm," I told him.

"I need to go apologize to her," he said, then he started walking down the sidewalk. After a few steps, he spun around and said, "Thanks again, Laurel. You're a good friend."

"Get out of here," I told him with a grin on my face.

He sprinted off. I took the elevator back to the third floor, but Charlie wasn't at our special table. I wondered if he'd already showed up, noticed that I wasn't there, and left. When I turned around, I almost bumped into my special guy.

"You're not going to study?" he asked.

"I already did."

"Me too. I was on my way out when I overheard somebody talking about love, and that made me think of you. So I came back to look for you one more time."

My heart stopped for a second. Love? That was a strong word. But that was the next step in our relationship, and I was ready for it. Still, I didn't want to push it. He hadn't actually said he was in love with me.

"I'm glad you double-checked," I told him, giving him a long hug.

I heard a female voice say, "Excuse me." I turned around and saw Jewels, her eyes checking out Charlie from top to bottom. "Aren't going to introduce me?" she asked coyly.

I cleared my throat. "Charlie, this is—"

"Jewels," she said, batting her eyes.

"Nice to meet you," Charlie said. He turned to me. "I've got to catch up with my friends, Lucy. See you tomorrow?"

"Same time, same place," I said as we embraced again.

After he walked away, Jewels said, "Who is that fine guy? And why'd he call you Lucy?"

I promised to tell her all about him as we walked home. But when we got back downstairs, the rest of the group was waiting for us. So I ended up telling them all about Charlie.

My friends told me how happy they were for me. I loved being in a sorority, and I hoped that when Charlie found out I was in one, he would like all of my friends.

———————

A week passed, and boy, was it long. I successfully made it through exams and practicing cheers. But it wasn't much fun.

"I might as well just quit," I told Payton one afternoon after spending hours trying to learn the cheerleading routines.

"Don't say that. You're going to get it. Whenever you do those flips across the gym, everyone wishes they could be like you. I know the cheerleaders want you on the squad."

"Thanks," I said, really wanting to believe what she said.

I trudged over to the vending machine, where I dug through my purse for some money.

"Need change?" Payton asked, handing me three quarters. I hugged her, promising I'd pay her back.

"You don't have to," she said.

"But I want to," I told her, putting the coins into the machine.

"How about instead you just go on that blind date with me? Tad's friend is so neat." She cracked a smile.

I had to admit my opinion of Tad had gone up when I saw him resist temptation and immediately go make things right with Payton. Maybe this close friend of his wasn't too bad.

I sighed. "OK," I mumbled, hoping she'd let me off the hook.

"This is gonna be great," she said, hugging me tightly.

"Don't make it too soon, though."

"OK. Whenever you think you're ready, let me know. It doesn't have to be tomorrow. Maybe sometime in the next week or so."

I shook my head. Payton grabbed her cell phone and dialed Tad. When she told him I'd agreed to the blind date, I started feeling guilty. How could I do this to Charlie? I had to tell him about it. I didn't want to be dishonest with him. Maybe it wouldn't matter to him. After all, there was no way I would like Tad's friend.

That night, at the library, I tried to think of the best way to tell Charlie about the blind date my roommate had conned me into agreeing to. But every time I started to tell him, I choked up.

"Is there something you want to talk about?" he finally asked.

"My roommate wants to set me up on a blind date," I blurted out.

"That's funny," he said. "My buddy has been trying to do the same thing for me."

"Really?" I said, amazed that he wasn't angry.

"I told him I'd do it."

I couldn't believe what Charlie was saying. He seemed to not even care how it would affect me for him to go out with someone else! Well, if he wanted to accept his friend's invitation, then I wasn't going to feel bad about doing it too.

I stood and started collecting my stuff.

"Did I say something wrong?" Charlie asked.

I continued trying to stack all my books, but they kept slipping out of my grasp.

Charlie helped me while he pleaded his case. "There's no way the girl is going to mean anything to me. She couldn't possibly compare to you. I just want to get my buddy off my back."

"Fine. Whatever," I said, snatching my books out of Charlie's hands. Though he'd told me exactly what I was planning to say to him, he didn't seem to have a problem with the idea.

"Why are you acting like this? Are you jealous? Come on, let's talk."

I stormed away from the table.

Charlie came up behind me at the elevator. "Please don't leave like this."

"I have to get ready for my date," I sneered. "And I don't think I want to see you until it's over." The elevator door slid open and I darted inside.

When I turned around he said, "If we care for each other, what's the big deal?"

I was glad the doors shut so I wouldn't have to answer the question.

When I walked into my dorm room, I saw Payton talking to Jewels. "I'm ready for that blind date anytime," I said.

"Great," Payton said. "You're gonna love this guy, I promise."

I jumped onto my bed and buried my head in my pillow.

"Come on," I heard Payton say to Jewels. "Let's go talk in your room."

After my friends left, I lay there thinking about Charlie. The more I thought about him going out with another girl, the more I felt like a balloon filled up with hot air and ready to pop.

Maybe he didn't like me as much as I liked him. Maybe we didn't need to get serious.

I silently recited a few psalms to try to calm myself down. Finally I realized that I didn't have to worry. God was in control. Maybe these blind dates would turn out to be just what Charlie and I needed to help us figure out how deep our feelings were for each other.

Being honest and open in our relationship was the only way to go. If another girl totally blew Charlie's mind, I would graciously let him go.

As for my own date, I decided to do my best to enjoy it. It was only one night. I felt sure nothing significant would happen.

I sat up and turned on the TV, jazzed to find a gymnastics meet. Our team was killing Alabama. Nadia was awesome. Summer did a great job on vault. I really felt happy for them.

The next morning, Nadia showed up at my door holding a large wicker basket full of fruit and candy. "This is for you," she said as she came in.

"What for?" I asked, setting it on the bed.

"The first day of cheerleading tryouts, of course. I want you to know I'm thinking about you. After you get called for the team, you can head back here and have a feast. I wish I could be here for you, but the team is heading out to LSU for another meet."

"I sure appreciate you," I told her as I gave her a big hug. Together we sorted through the munchies in the basket.

"The whole team misses you, Laurel. We feel you with us in spirit."

"Thanks," I said, feeling all choked up. "How is everyone doing spiritually?"

"Several of the girls have been asking about the Bible, and I'm actually witnessing to them."

"That's awesome," I said.

"I think so." She gave me a big hug. "I've got to get going."

"Thanks for the basket."

"You're welcome," she said.

Two hours later Payton and I were holding hands in the locker room. We were dressed in our red shorts and white polo shirts with a number on each of our backs. She opened a prayer and I closed it.

After we finished asking God for His blessings during our tryouts, two girls approached us.

The redhead with the number fifty-six on her back introduced herself as Beatrice. Her friend, a petite girl with short jet-black hair and number fifty-seven on her back, told us her name was Kathy.

"We saw you guys praying," Beatrice said.

"Yeah," Payton said, her back stiff. "What about it?"

"We were just wondering," Kathy said, "if you'd mind praying for us too."

"Sure," Payton said with a wide smile.

The four of us held hands. "Father," I prayed, "we come to You now with a little nervousness. We're about to step out on the court, and we need Your strength and guidance. We give the results to You." I took a little breath. "Lord, I don't really know where these two girls are in their walk with Christ, but I want to pray for their salvation. I know their heart's desire is to be cheerleaders, but that pales in comparison to what You've got for us. Lord, don't let us lose sight of Your will. Payton and I want others to know You, and if cheerleading can help us witness to people, we're ready to be used by You. Amen."

After we all looked up, Beatrice gave me a big hug. She was crying. "I hope I do good."

"I'm sure you will," I assured her.

"I don't know," she said between sniffles. "I'm not sure I'm Georgia material."

"Don't say that," Payton said. "You can't be any worse than Laurel." She winked at me.

"That's for sure," I said, trying to lighten the mood.

When the names were called for the first round of cuts, Kathy made it, but Beatrice didn't. It broke my heart when I saw her shuffle away. I hoped she remembered what I'd said in my prayer about cheerleading being nothing compared to what God wanted for us.

To my delight, Payton and I both made the first round.

"I can't believe it," I screamed.

"Me either," she screamed back.

When I asked her how we should celebrate, she said, "The blind date, of course. I made it for tonight."

"Why didn't you tell me?" I shrieked.

She put her hands on her hips. "I didn't want you to lose focus on the tryouts."

I sighed.

"So, where are we going?" I asked as we headed back to our room. "Do I have to get all dressed up?"

"No," she said. "We're just going to Pizza Hut."

"Good. I'm starved."

As I got dressed, I pretended I was going out with Charlie. That helped me pick out something cute. I settled on blue jeans and an orange knit top.

As Payton drove to the restaurant, I started sweating and fidgeting.

"What's wrong?" my roommate asked.

I wiped my forehead with a tissue from my purse. "I've been wanting to tell you something for a long time."

"What?" she asked, looking at me like she was scared.

"All the time I've been spending at the library lately . . ."

Payton gave me a concerned glance. "Have you been seeing somebody?"

I nodded.

"You've been holding out on me? Well, this guy can't be too special if you agreed to go on this date."

"I only said yes because you pestered me so much," I complained. "Besides, my guy is going out on a date too." I sniffed. "So I guess you're right. It can't be too special."

"Girl, forget about him. I'm telling you, you're gonna like this guy tonight."

"Just don't push too hard, OK?"

"Of course not."

The Pizza Hut was crowded but we found Tad and his friend sitting at a booth in the far corner. I couldn't see my date's face because his back was to us. He didn't even have the decency to get up when we arrived.

Tad stood and gave Payton a hug. Then she turned to his friend. "Hey, Casey," she said, "this is my friend Laurel."

When Payton stepped out of the way, I finally saw my blind date. I couldn't believe my eyes. It was Charlie. He looked just as stunned as I felt. After a few seconds of shock, he jumped up and hugged me tight.

"Do you guys know each other?" Tad asked.

"This is my guy from the library," I told Payton.

"But you said his name was Charlie," she said.

We sat in the booth and the waitress took our order. Then Charlie and I explained to Payton and Tad how we met.

To my astonishment, I discovered that "Charlie" was actually Casey Hanson, the kicker for our football team!

"Why didn't you tell him who you were, Laurel?" Payton asked.

"He said he didn't like sorority girls," I said.

Charlie put his arm around my back. "You're in a sorority? I thought you were an athlete."

"I'm both," I told him.

I found out that he liked me the first day we met, when I started defending Casey Hanson to the guys in the library. Since I'd talked about what jerks most athletes were, he didn't want to tell me who he really was.

Payton grinned at both of us. "So you didn't think he liked sorority girls, and you didn't think she liked football players, so both of you kept your identities a secret." She glanced at her boyfriend. "Good thing Tad and I realized you were made for each other."

The waitress arrived with our pizzas and we dug in. After a few slices and some friendly banter, Casey looked at me. "So now that you know who I am, are we gonna make this thing official? Think you can handle dating a football player?"

"Oh, yes," I told him, batting my eyes at him. He kissed me softly.

I couldn't believe I had been going out with Casey Hanson, the guy I'd been admiring from afar. But I knew he was just what God wanted for me because he loved the Lord.

That night was the best blind date I'd ever had. I learned much more about Casey. It was fun being with the guy who owned my heart, especially now that we knew all about each other.

Payton wiped her mouth on a napkin and grinned at us. "You guys are such a cute couple."

After we smiled at each other, Casey made a toast to great relationships. Tad then toasted to Payton and me for making the first round of cheerleading tryouts. I felt so relaxed. No stress. It was such a joy releasing the pressure.

f o u r t e e n

mending
broken hearts

1 aurel, huh?" Casey said as he stood by the front door of
my dormitory. "I like that a lot better than Lucy."

"I like Casey a lot better than Charlie," I said, smiling.

We discussed more facts about each other. Filling in the details made the picture I had of him even better.

I asked him why he didn't like sorority girls. He told me that in his senior year of high school he dated a girl who went to the University of Washington after graduation. When she got there, she joined a sorority and dropped him, which broke his heart.

"I'd like to prove that your impression of sorority girls is wrong," I told him.

"And how do you plan on doing that?" he asked with a grin.

"My spring dance is coming up and I want you to escort me. Jewels has already told everyone I have a hot guy, and they all expect us to be there. When they find out you're Casey Hanson, they'll all want your autograph."

He laughed. "Do I have to wear a tux?"

"Yes," I said. "And I know you'll be handsome in it."

Jewels and Robyn brushed past us and went into the dorm as if they didn't even see us. Their faces looked distraught. I wondered what they were so bummed out about.

"Those are my suite mates," I said. "I'd better find out what's wrong."

"Go ahead."

I kissed Casey on the cheek and gave him a hug, then bounded up to my room.

When I got there, I raced through the bathroom to the other side of our suite. I found my two friends sprawled on their beds. Jewels was crying and Robyn had an angry glare on her face. What was going on?

Then it dawned on me. Final tryouts for the dance team had been that day. Obviously, it hadn't gone well.

Before I could say anything, I heard Payton come into our room. I went back through the bathroom and told her about our suite mates.

"Payton, you've got to say something to them," I said, tugging her toward their room.

As we reached the door, my phone rang. It was my mom. Payton went into the next room to talk to our friends while I chatted on the phone.

Everything at home was in order. My dad wasn't down any longer. "Your talk helped him heal a little," my mother said.

"It wasn't me," I told her. "It was God using me."

"I've never seen your dad lead the church with such authority. The Lord is really working in his life."

Mom and I chatted a little while longer. After we hung up, Robyn came in. "I need to talk to you."

"Sure," I said as I sat on my bed.

Robyn stood beside me. "Please don't say anything to

Payton, but I really like Dakari and I think he likes me. I know Dakari used to be her boyfriend, and I think he still likes her. But we've been spending a lot of time together at recruiting and all. And we talked a lot after his brother got shot at that club, and that got us pretty close." She fidgeted with the hem of her top. "He asked me to go out with him tonight for ice cream," she blurted out.

"That sounds like a date to me," I said. "What are you going to do?"

"What do you think I should do?"

Payton and I had decided to let our exes go. And I knew Robyn would be a great girl for Dakari. But I also knew Payton wouldn't want me to interfere.

"All I can tell you is to trust your heart. I still think about Branson sometimes, so I know how Payton might feel." I shrugged. "You should just talk to her."

"Thanks. I may do that." She looked up at me. "But until I do, you won't say anything, right?"

"I promise."

Suddenly, Robyn got really excited. "Hey, how were your cheerleading tryouts?"

"Payton and I both made it," I announced.

"That's great," she said, giving me a congratulations hug. "I'm really happy for you." After the hug, her eyes looked sad.

"You didn't make the dance team, did you?" I said gently.

"Oh, I made it."

"Then why are you so bummed out?"

"Jewels was better than me, but she didn't make it. I think the only reason I made the team is because I'm black. I told her I'd let her have my spot. She said I shouldn't do that because she's not sure that she was next on the list."

"You made the team because the judges thought you were qualified," I assured her.

"I wish I believed that," Robyn said as she dropped her head.

"Why are you so down on yourself?"

"I don't know," she mumbled. "I guess I still feel kind of guilty about the abortion. Sometimes I feel like I did the right thing, and other times I think maybe I should have had the baby."

"It's done. In the past. You've got to let go of the pain." I held her hand and she let out a few sobs, then cried in my arms. After a few moments, she pulled herself together.

"How are things going between you and Jackson?" I asked her.

"I hate him," she seethed. "You were right when you told me I shouldn't change schools for a guy. In all the time I've been here, he has never once acknowledged me as his girl-friend. I know I need to get over him and move on. But I think I need to heal from all the hurt Jackson caused me be-fore I even think about getting into another relationship."

"You're right," I said. "And God is the only One who can help you heal."

"I think He's doing that by sending me Dakari to talk to."

"You can always talk to me about stuff like this," I said.

"But you're way down the road that leads to heaven. Dakari and Jewels and I are all just starting out."

"Sounds like you and Jewels have gotten pretty tight," I said, remembering how much they'd both fought against rooming together.

"We've talked a lot," Robyn said, staring down at her hands. "We've really been able to encourage each other."

I gave her a big hug.

She stood. "I've got to get ready. Dakari's coming to pick me up at seven o'clock."

I gave her a smug frown. "So you didn't really need my advice. You already made plans to go out with him."

Robyn shrugged. Then she exited through the bathroom as Payton entered.

My roommate sat on my bed. "Jewels is really upset."

"Why?" I asked.

"She's embarrassed about not making the dance team. And that formal is coming up and she doesn't have anyone to take her."

"Really?" That surprised me since all the guys seemed to love her.

"She said she'd like to have Branson take her, but she admires you too much to make a move on him. Maybe you should call him and ask him to invite her."

"I don't know," I said.

"Hey, it's not like you need him anymore. You've got Casey Hanson."

I wanted to ask her how she would feel if Robyn went out with Dakari. But Robyn had asked me to keep her confidence, so I didn't say a word.

Payton got up and rummaged through her drawers. "Have you seen my red top?"

"Which one?" I asked, chuckling. "You have a dozen."

"I know," she said as she peered into the closet. "My mom sends them to me. She loves the Delta sorority, and red's their color."

"Have you thought about pledging them?"

She smiled. "I might. They're actually pretty cool."

"Maybe you and Robyn could pledge together."

Payton frowned. "I think she wants to be an AKA. But we can't pledge either one till next year, so we've got time to think about it."

I opened my closet door and pulled out a red top.

"Is this the one you're searching for?" I asked.

"Yes," she said, grabbing it out of my hands. "When I washed clothes the other day, I ran out of room and hung some stuff on your side. You don't mind, do you?"

"Of course not." I watched her hold the shirt in front of her and check herself out in the mirror. "Going somewhere special?"

"Tad and I are going out to get some ice cream."

I gulped as Payton made a quick change. There was only one ice cream shop in the neighborhood, so there was no doubt that's where Robyn and Dakari would be. I wanted to tell Payton not to go there, but before I could figure out what to say, she headed out the door.

Knowing there was nothing I could do about the situation, I decided to focus on trying to help Jewels get a date for the formal.

It wouldn't be easy to ask Branson to take her out. It wasn't that I wanted him for myself. I had a great guy, and he was a lot better for me than Branson could ever be. But I'd been having a hard time thinking about my ex-boyfriend dating somebody else. I needed to release my past. Maybe hooking Branson up with Jewels would help me get over the lingering feelings I had for him.

"What do you think?" Jewels asked as she sashayed into my room on the night of spring formal.

I gasped. She was absolutely stunning in a long, form-fitting gown with a low neckline and a slit up her right thigh. "You look beautiful. I'm sure Branson will be pleased."

"Thanks," she said, beaming and twirling. "And thanks again for double-dating with me and Branson." She went to the bathroom to put on more lipstick.

I couldn't believe Casey had suggested the four of us go to the dance together. He said he wanted to meet the guy who used to have my affection.

"Don't get me wrong," Jewels said after she blotted her lips. "I'm still hurt over Kelly, but I'm really excited about spending time with Branson."

The dorm monitor knocked on my door. "Casey Hanson is here for you," Judy said. The twinkle in her eye told me she knew who he was and maybe felt a little jealous. I figured I'd get a lot of that.

When Jewels and I reached the front door of the dorm,

Casey was standing there, looking gorgeous in a black tuxedo.

When Casey saw us he said, "You ladies are stunning." He leaned over and kissed me on the cheek.

I blushed. "And you're so handsome you could give the *GQ* models a run for their money."

He offered an arm to Jewels and escorted us both to his car, where he opened the doors for both of us. "You'll have to tell me where to go to pick up Branson."

I was all set to give directions to the fraternity house, but Jewels said, "Go straight and then turn right at the stop sign. When you get to the top of the hill, his house will be on the left."

When we pulled up outside the fraternity house, we saw at least a dozen guys in tuxedos standing on the front porch.

"Casey," Jewels asked, "would you go get him for me, please?"

He turned around and stared at her. "I don't know which one is him."

"Just ask for Branson Price," Jewels said.

"Branson Price?" A light shone in Casey's eyes as he peered at me. "I didn't know he was your ex." As Casey jumped out of the car, it occurred to me that I had never mentioned Branson's last name.

When Casey came back with Branson, the two were laughing like old friends.

Of course, I thought. *They both play football!*

"This is going to be interesting," Jewels said, grinning.

Branson hopped into the back of the car with Jewels. He smiled as he said hello to her and then to me. Casey got in and winked at me.

As we headed for Athens, Jewels asked, "So, how do you guys know each other?"

"We were recruited at the same time," Branson said in a bragging tone.

"You play football?" Jewels asked.

"He sure does," I said. "He was the quarterback at our high school. He was really awesome."

Casey's cold glance told me he didn't like hearing me sing Branson's praises. I leaned back in the seat and hushed up.

"I wondered what happened to you after tryouts," Casey said, watching Branson in the rearview mirror. "I figured you must have signed with another school."

"No," Branson said. "Georgia has always been my dream. But I got hurt in my senior year and I'm still not really over it. I want to be out there with you guys, but there's not much I can do."

"If you're healed by next season, you should try for a walk-on. Our new coach is making everybody really earn their positions. He told everyone on the team that whoever plays the best will get the starting spots, regardless of seniority."

I was thrilled that Casey was giving Branson hope for his dreams.

When we arrived at Lake Lanier, several cars were lined up to pull into the parking lot. When we got out of ours, I tried to put a little distance between Branson and Jewels, and Casey and me. I didn't want to remain a foursome all night.

After Branson and Jewels walked away arm in arm, Casey and I strolled into the beautifully decorated ballroom. The minute we crossed the threshold, a group of girls left their dates to swarm around Casey, all asking for his autograph. I stepped aside and let him please his fans.

After a few minutes I found myself standing next to Branson. Jewels was in the throng of Casey's admirers.

"Do you really like him?" Branson asked me. I could tell from his tone that he was jealous.

"A lot," I replied, hoping he could be happy for me.

"You're beautiful," he said as he placed his hand on my arm.

I pulled back from him.

"I wish you'd give me another chance." He nodded toward Casey. "A guy like that can't be faithful to you."

"How can you say that? You don't know him."

"I can see who's getting his attention," Branson said, nodding at the girls surrounding my boyfriend.

"Casey's love for God will keep him true to me."

Branson stepped between me and my date. "You already tried the Christian boyfriend thing, Laurel, and it didn't work out."

"Casey's not Foster," I argued.

"So you're telling me there's no chance for us?" He grabbed my arm and stared deep into my eyes. The intensity on his face frightened me.

Casey appeared and grasped Branson's shoulder. "Don't touch her like that," he whispered through clenched teeth.

"Excuse me," Branson said, jerking his arm from Casey. "We were just talking."

Casey glared at Branson. "Whatever you have to say to Laurel, you can say in front of me."

I noticed several people watching us. "It's no big deal, Casey," I whispered, trying to put out the fire before it got too hot.

"I was a jerk to her in high school," Branson said. "But I know she still loves me, and I want another chance."

"It's over between us," I told Branson firmly. "I'm in love with Casey. You have to let go of your feelings for me."

Casey placed his arm around my waist. Tears welled up in Branson's eyes.

"I'm sorry," I said quietly.

"Don't worry about me," he said in a gravely voice. "I'll get over you just fine." He stomped off through the gawking crowd.

My eyes met Casey's. He kissed my forehead.

Jewels walked up to us. "What was all that about?"

"Branson doesn't want to see me with someone else."

"Sounds like he's hurting. I'll go talk to him." Jewels lifted the hem of her gown and headed toward Branson.

I was glad she wasn't upset that her date had come on to me. Someone she cared about was hurting and she wanted to be a friend to him. She was placing someone else's needs in front of her own, and that told me she had done a lot of growing. The Holy Spirit was working in her life.

Casey led me to a quiet corner. "So you're in love with me, huh?" he teased.

I didn't respond with words. I just kissed him softly on the lips.

"I realize Branson hurt you a lot. But I want you to know I won't ever let you down. I will always be true to what we have. Our relationship is built on a solid foundation, and with God's strength I promise to always try to make you happy."

I hugged him with tears in my eyes. I didn't know what was going to happen between Casey and me, but God had brought us to this point and that was reason to celebrate.

I thought about Jewels, Robyn, and Payton, and my high school friends Meagan and Brittany. I hoped they would turn all of their problems over to the Lord, like I had. With God as their doctor, they would no longer have to be mending broken hearts.

fɪ f t e ɴ

knowing
i'm blessed

"Can you believe we're national champions again?" a short guy with a large stomach and a receding hairline said to me as we stood in front of the gym waiting for the gymnastics team to return from Alabama. "That's the third time in five years."

"I think it's wonderful," I said. "The Gym Dawgs deserve the championship. They worked really hard this season."

I had wanted to attend the meet personally, but I'd been too busy with sorority stuff and cheerleading tryouts. Besides, I couldn't really afford the flight. So I'd watched the meet on TV. Nadia had earned all tens on every rotation she did except the vault. I couldn't wait to give her a big hug.

Finally the bus rolled up, and the fans cheered. When the gymnastics team got off, they stepped onto a red carpet that had been rolled out between the curb and the gym entrance. As the gymnasts climbed off the bus, they found friends and family in the crowd.

When Nadia saw me, she hugged me tight.

"I was praying for you," I said over the noise.

"God blessed me in a mighty way," she said. "I was able to be a light, Laurel. I won over three girls to Christ."

"That's awesome!" I hugged her tightly.

Summer came up and smiled at me. "Did you see our girl win first place?" She patted Nadia on the back.

Then Marcy walked up to us. She was one of the gymnasts who'd been rude to me. "I'm sorry I gave you such a hard time when you tried to get on the team, Laurel," she said sweetly. "I was wrong."

"Thanks," I said, hardly able to acknowledge that this was the same girl who'd said all those hateful things to me such a short time ago.

"Nadia showed me that I need Jesus," she explained. "I accepted Christ, and now I want to be different. I want to live for Him."

I smiled. "That's great news."

Coach Burrows came up to us. "Laurel, it's good to see you. Nadia told me you've been praying for us all. Your prayers bonded this team together, and we got a ring to show for it. Thanks."

I was humbled. My heart really felt good hearing such appreciation. Finally I realized my role for the team this year was to be their prayer warrior.

"Nadia told me you're trying out for cheerleading," the coach said. "I'm sure you'll make the squad, but if you don't, I hope you'll try out for gymnastics next year."

"I'll remember that," I said.

Coach Burrows and the Gym Dawgs started heading into the gym, followed by their friends, families, and fans.

Tugging Nadia's hand, I asked, "What did God do to soften Marcy's heart?"

Nadia's eyes lit up. "He used you," she said with a grin.

"Me?"

"When you got cut from the team, and you didn't act

jealous or anything, that got me to thinking about my own attitudes. In the past, whenever I excelled and my friends didn't, they got jealous. You didn't do that. So I decided to start encouraging Marcy whenever she did something well. That broke the bitterness between us and we started getting along really well. We even decided to have a weekly prayer and worship time together, and pretty soon most of the team wanted to join."

I shook my head.

"Come on," Nadia said, glancing at the gym, which was filling up with people. "Let's get inside."

I squeezed Nadia's hand. "I have to go."

Her eyes grew wide. "You're not staying for the big celebration?"

"I wish I could," I said, "but I've got cheerleading tryouts tomorrow, so I need to get a good night's sleep."

"I understand," she said. "Thanks for being here."

After a hug, Nadia joined her teammates and fans in the gym. As I started back toward my dorm, someone yelled from behind, "You shouldn't be walking by yourself after dark."

I turned around and saw Casey.

"How did you know I was here?" I asked.

"Payton told me," he said. "It wasn't easy finding you in that big crowd." He chuckled. "I think the gymnastics team has more fans than the football team."

"I'm glad you found me," I said, wrapping my arms around his waist.

"Me too," he said.

"I wanted to be on that team so bad," I said, gazing back at the gym.

"But you were," he said.

I looked up at him in confusion.

"Your prayers made a difference for them, just like when you were praying for me on the football field." He lifted my chin and placed a kiss on my cheek.

I smiled. Then we walked hand in hand to my dorm.

"So, tomorrow's the big day, huh?" he said.

"Yeah," I replied, shivering as I thought about the cheer-leading tryouts.

"I've got something for you," he said, handing me a card from his shorts pocket.

I opened the envelope and pulled out a handwritten note. It said:

Laurel,

Please join us for breakfast. You can't try out on an empty stomach. Hope to see you at our home at 8 a.m.

Laurie Randolph

"Oh, my gosh," I said, the invitation quivering in my hands. "This is from the head football coach's wife."

"Since my parents live so far away, the coach took me under his wing. The Randolphs are like my second parents. I've told them how wonderful you are and they want to meet you. Please say you'll come."

"Of course I will," I said. "It sounds fun."

The Randolph home was a six-thousand-square-foot ranch house. When I walked through the double-door entrance, I saw a circular mahogany table with a large bouquet of fresh flowers on it. Behind the foyer was an enormous dining room with a view of the garden in the backyard. The table was set with elegant china plates, crystal water goblets, and sparkling silverware.

Coach Randolph encouraged me to make myself at home and told me how glad he and his wife were to meet me.

After we sat at the table, Mrs. Randolph said grace. Then two servers brought out our meal.

Throughout breakfast, Coach Randolph talked about

God. "I want to win as many games as possible," he said, "so I can stay at UGA and work on my real agenda, which is making sure all my athletes hear the gospel and have the opportunity to become saved."

"My dad's a pastor," I said, "and he was real excited when he heard you were going to be our new coach. He said he went to school with you at the University of Arkansas."

"I knew your last name rang a bell," he said with a grin. "Is your father Dave Shadrach?"

I nodded.

"I was quarterback at U of A when your dad was a sophomore." He wiped his mouth with a linen napkin and leaned back in his chair. "I'll have to visit his church sometime."

"I'm sure he'd like that," I said.

"Please write down the address for us before you leave," Mrs. Randolph requested.

"I will," I promised.

Coach Randolph turned to Casey. "There's something in the den I need to show you." The two men excused themselves.

Mrs. Randolph offered me a cup of tea. I gladly accepted and began to gather the dirty plates.

"Oh, don't worry about those," she said. "The maid will clean up. Let's sit and chat for a while."

I followed her to the living room, where a silver pot and delicate china cups were sitting on an oval coffee table.

"Casey's a sweetie," Mrs. Randolph said as she poured the tea. "He's the model Christian."

"I like him a lot," I admitted.

"My husband and I haven't been blessed with children, but I've often felt like a mom to the football players. Casey especially. I'm very happy that you two are friends."

I smiled. "So am I."

"Casey tells me you're nervous about the cheerleading tryouts."

I stared at the steaming liquid in my cup. "I had some problems with the dance portion, but my best friend has been helping me out. I just hope I can stay calm enough to do the routine."

"I cheered at Arkansas," she said. "At my first tryouts, I messed up three times. Needless to say, I didn't make the squad. But the next year I tried again, and that time I made it."

"Thanks for sharing that with me," I said, then sipped the tea.

She placed her hand on my shoulder. "From what Casey has told me about you, I can tell you're a fighter. God's got something special for you. It might include becoming a cheerleader, or it might not. But you're a charming young lady, and I see God's Spirit shining all over you. So just go out there today and have fun."

"I'll do my best," I said. "I don't want to let Casey down."

"Actually," Mrs. Randolph said, "I think he would prefer that you don't make the squad."

I looked up at her.

"If you become a cheerleader, you won't have as much time for him." She chuckled. "Then again, with all the practice my husband's going to have him doing, you'll need your own life."

That afternoon, as I stood in front of the judges for the cheerleading squad, I could still hear Mrs. Randolph's words: *"The Holy Spirit is shining all over you."*

I realized she wasn't just talking about me being a cheerleader. What really mattered was being a child of the King.

The dance steps that had given me difficulty for months came easily. The cheer I thought I'd never get was flawless. When my partner did stunts with me, I flew up into the air light as a feather and landed as gracefully as a ballerina.

On one of the moves I knew backward and forward, I tripped. That made me want to cry. But, I told myself, mistakes happen. I just got up and did thirteen back handsprings.

"That was awesome," my partner whispered to me.

Payton shined as well. Her spunk and excitement were contagious. The judges seemed impressed as I watched them enjoy her performance.

My confidence subsided a little as Payton and I waited for the results. As we sat on the bleachers awaiting the announcement, we held hands and prayed.

"Lord," Payton said quietly as we huddled close, "please block out all the drama and let us focus on You. Even if neither of us makes it on the squad, let us be missionaries for You at this school."

We said a quick amen when the judge asked for everyone's attention.

"When I call your name," the judge said, "please come to the center of the court."

Payton and I held each other's hands.

The judge announced that the girls who'd made the team were Becky, Tristan, Kayla, Carly, and Laurel. Whoever was sitting behind me pushed me toward center court, but all I could think about was that I hadn't heard Payton's name. I didn't want to go up there if my roommate didn't make the squad wit me. But before I got to center court, I heard the coach announce Payton's name too.

We all hugged one another, and Payton and I cried tears of joy.

Then I saw Kathy shuffling out of the gym, her shoulders slumped. She hadn't made the final cut. I prayed God would help her accept the decision and look forward to His will for her.

As Payton and I hugged each other again, I saw Casey and Tad standing near the bleachers, each of them holding a bouquet of roses. I touched Payton on the arm and pointed to them. We dashed over to our guys.

"We heard the announcements," Tad said. "Congratulations."

"What were you two going to do if we didn't make it?" Payton asked after taking a deep whiff of her flowers.

"Then the roses would have been 'We love you anyway' flowers," Casey answered.

"You're wonderful," I said, hugging him tightly.

Then I saw my parents standing near the entrance of the gym. After I hugged and kissed them, I asked why they were there.

"We came to support you, of course," my mom said.

"Who's this?" Dad asked, eyeing Casey.

I introduced my father to my boyfriend.

"It's a pleasure to meet you, sir," Casey said.

"I've seen you play," my father told him. "You're a fine kicker."

"Thank you, sir," Casey said, almost blushing.

"I saw a story ESPN did on you last year," my dad added. "Apparently you're quite a scholar too."

My dad and Casey started talking about Coach Randolph. Casey said he'd heard great things about my father's athletic ability when he was in college.

When a little boy asked Casey for his autograph, my dad whispered in my ear, "I like him."

I beamed.

I looked around for Payton and found her mom and mine jabbering by the bleachers. Then I saw Branson staring at me from center court.

"I'll be right back," I told my parents and Casey.

When I reached Branson, he said, "I'm really proud of you."

"Thanks," I said.

"I talked to Coach Randolph about trying for a walk-on next year. He says I have a good shot."

"That's great."

Stepping closer, Branson said, "Laurel, I know I messed up by treating you the way I did. When I wanted to go down the wrong road, you stayed with the Lord. And He

160

has blessed you for it." Branson looked at Casey. "He's a great guy. I approve of you being with him."

I laughed on the inside. I hardly needed his approval. But I was glad he was happy for me. It was his way of saying we could be friends.

"I've been having quiet times with God over the last couple of weeks," he told me.

I took his hand. "Keep growing in your walk with God. A relationship with Him will fill you like nothing else can."

"I'm beginning to realize that," he told me. "It's not going to be easy, but I'm planning to walk with Him."

"How about you and Jewels?" I asked.

"She's nice. But right now I need to concentrate on my relationship with God."

"Wise choice."

"Brittany will never believe you're a Georgia cheerleader. She'll be mad you held out and didn't cheer with her in high school. Then again, she wouldn't have wanted you to compete with her for the most popular girl in school."

"That's Brit," I said, and we shared a laugh.

Branson's face grew serious. "Your family's waiting. You'd better go be with them."

As I walked back toward Casey and my folks, I felt as though Branson had released me for good. But he and I would always have a connection in Christ. I couldn't wait to see what great things God was going to do in our lives.

"So, Miss Cheerleader," Jewels said, "are you going to move into the sorority house now?"

Jewels had been begging me to move with her to the Alpha Gamma Delta house for our sophomore year.

I sat up on my bed. "You've got to stop making snide remarks like that."

"What did I say?" she asked.

"Referring to me as Miss Cheerleader is rude."

"I don't think so," Jewels said. "I'm proud of you for making the squad. I've told all my friends about you becoming a cheerleader."

"Thanks. That means a lot to me."

"Julie Anne says she can pull some strings to make sure we get a room together."

"I've got to talk to Payton first," I said.

I did want to move to the sorority house eventually. It would be a little cheaper than the dorm, and we'd have a cook and a maid. But Payton was special to me, and I thanked God we'd been roommates during my freshman year.

"With you as my roommate, I know I'd stay on the straight and narrow," she said with a smile.

I patted Jewels's back. "Thanks for being a real sister."

The next day Payton and I went to Six Flags in Atlanta with Casey and Tad to celebrate making the cheerleading squad.

My roommate and I were sitting on a wooden bench underneath a flowered arch, waiting for our guys to get us hot dogs, when I started thinking about what my life would be like if I moved out of the dorm. I didn't know how I was going to tell Payton I didn't want to room with her anymore. I felt horrible. I couldn't even look her in the eye.

"What are you thinking about?" she probed.

I told Payton my thoughts about the following year's living arrangements.

To my surprise, Payton told me she wasn't planning to room with me. She and Robyn had found an apartment they were going to share with some other girls.

We looked at each other and started laughing.

"Since we'll be cheering together," she said, "we'll still see plenty of each other."

I had gotten worked up over nothing. God had already

figured everything out for me. I felt grateful that I had a Savior who loved me so much.

We enjoyed the rest of our day at the amusement park, and we talked about God all the way back. We had a major praise time in the car, all of us shouting about how good God had been to us.

The first time I put on my red pleated skirt and red top with the word *Georgia* on it, a huge grin covered my face. I couldn't have wiped it off no matter what.

During the first game Payton and I cheered for, Tad rushed 110 yards and Casey kicked a fifty-two-yard field goal.

Between handsprings, I thought about the last couple of years of my life. I had been through a lot, but I had grown so much. The Lord was with me all the way. He'd taught me that He wanted me to remain pure. That He wanted me to be excited about His Word. And that alcohol and drugs were not for me. He had led me to the people I needed to be hooked up with so they could know Him too.

I learned that I was special because I was His child, and my life needed to be spent witnessing. I had great friends and wonderful parents. And now I had a special guy. I knew my heavenly Father would always be there for me.

I felt so great about my life, I did twenty-four back handsprings in a row. The crowd cheered. I waved at the fans and took a bow.

What a great feeling it is, knowing I'm blessed.

Purity Reigns

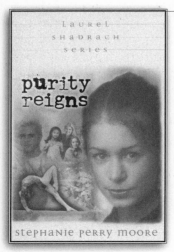

ISBN: 0-8024-4035-5

Laurel Shadrach is looking forward to her senior year being picture perfect! Her optimism turns sour when Branson begins to pressure her. She wants to keep the man she loves, but making a choice between obeying God and giving in to the desires of her flesh is difficult. Will Laurel let her desires for Branson come between her and God? Will the pressure she feels from Branson destroy her relationships with her family and friends? Will Laurel have the courage to say no to the man she loves?

Totally Free

There is never a dull moment in the ever-changing events of Laurel's life as she finds herself dealing with the effects of alcohol abuse on friends, family, and a community; a brother who is controlled by the excitement of gambling; and the peer pressures of giving in to sexual urges. Will Laurel continue to bear this heavy burden of secrecy and tolerance alone? Will the Lord show Himself faithful even in these difficult situations?

ISBN: 0-8024-4036-3

Equally Yoked

Laurel Shadrach's world may be a lot of things, but it's never boring. The last few weeks of her senior year are packed with gymnastics meets, parties, final exams, and family. But life topples Laurel's neatly stacked pyramid of plans. Laurel has always clung to faith in a loving God. But a jumble of disappointments and tragedies has shaken her to her foundations. Will her faith stand up to the pressure? Will God prove Himself good and kind even in the worst times life can offer?

ISBN: 0-8024-4037-1

Absolutely Worthy

Laurel's roommate, Payton Skky, is also a believer and a welcome friend. Too soon, though, a suddenly insecure Laurel falls under the influence of her suitemate Jewels. It wouldn't be so bad, except Jewels is prejudiced against African-American Payton, cruel to her own roommate Anna, and absolutely obsessed with the sorority rush.

When Laurel decides to rush the Alpha Gams with Jewels, she has some choices to make about her personal conduct, her true friendships, and her gymnastics future. Will Laurel come to realize her true identity in Christ?

ISBN: 0-8024-4038-X

MOODY
PUBLISHERS

THE NAME YOU CAN TRUST.

1-800-678-6928 www.MoodyPublishers.org

FINALLY SURE TEAM

ACQUIRING EDITOR:
Greg Thornton

COPY EDITOR:
Kathy Ide

BACK COVER COPY:
Julie-Allyson Ieron, Joy Media

COVER DESIGN:
Ragont Design

INTERIOR DESIGN:
Ragont Design

PRINTING AND BINDING:
Bethany Press International

The typeface for the text of this book is
Berkeley